The Lying of

Our Youth

William S. Carpenter

(Cover photo by Wes Hicks)

In the foothills of the Southern Appalachian Mountains sits a community festooned with verdant fields, picturesque lakes, laurel thickets, clapboard houses and moocows. The Scots-Irish settlers named the area Fonta Flora and for generations it subsisted on the sweat of men working plowshares, milking cows, making moonshine, and the fiery rhetoric that emanated from the Protestant pulpits that pepper the area. In the first decades of the twentieth century the powers that be made a concerted effort to bring industry to the area. Textile mills and manufacturing plants emerged to bring about the demise of family farming and deliver a modicum of monetary security to those destitute souls. That was the social norm for many decades until those in power decided to outsource the jobs and retool the locals for jobs and careers which didn't exist. That event caused a great upheaval in the lives of the Fonta Florans . A deep recession set in that resulted in them losing their homes, which, in turn, led to a massive influx of people from wealthier locales seeking to buy up the cheap property. When the gentrification started, and the town became unrecognizable, most of the locals just threw up their hands and went off to once again work the fields and milk the cows. Some went off to work in different climes, while others marched off to dead end jobs, but a tiny few decided to go their own way....

1

Catawba woke up and climbed out of bed and headed for the kitchen. He turned on the coffee pot and took off towards the front door. He unlocked the deadbolt and stepped out into the warm air of the morning. He walked across the porch to one of the brick columns and leaned up against it and stood there listening as the owls called out in vernal amorosity near the lake. When the owls quieted down and died away he went back inside and headed for the kitchen. He poured himself a cup of coffee and sipped on it as he walked around the room seeing what he needed to get from town.

He left near midmorning, driving to town on the hazy and bustling roads. He pulled into the Fonta Flora Farmers Market to find a hive of people going to and fro with their reusable cloth bags. He got out of his car and looked out at the mercantile circus of farmers selling blackberries, quail eggs, wildflower honey, muscadine wine, Italian kale, microgreens and an assortment of other locally sourced items.

He shut the car door and took off walking through the mass of people. He walked down to the end of the merchants and stopped in front of the goat cheese booth. He looked at the whiteboard and read the day's offerings. As the line disappeared he stepped up to the farmer's table.

"Yes, I would like a pound of blueberry chevre ."

"That's a good choice Catawba ," the farmer said as he reached into the cooler and brought a plastic tub. "We use our own blueberries in the process."

"How much?"

"Twelve."

He counted out the paper bills and passed them over to him. The farmer took the money, put the chevre in a paper poke, and thanked him. He took the poke and headed back through the long line of merchants. He stopped in the middle of the market to watch as barefoot hipsters and hillbillies danced around to the music of an old man playing a dobro.

When the song finished he walked on to the other end of the market and bought a pint jar of rhubarb jam and exchanged pleasantries with the seller. Then he headed back up the small hill to his car as more droves of people descended upon the market.

He left and drove across town to the big box grocery store. He pulled into the parking lot to find the place crowded and the buggies scattered to the wind. He got out and went inside the store and got the last buggy out of the stall and went through the double doors and started. He snaked through the aisles with celerity, checking things off his list as he went. When he had everything he needed he headed up to the checkout lanes. He unloaded the buggy and the cashier rang the items up. She told him the total and he started fingering through his wallet. As he handed her the money he noticed his old boss loading up a cart in the lane in front of him.

"Here you go," she said.

"Thank you."

He pocketed the change, picked up the bags, and walked up beside the man.

"How's it going these days?"

"Oh hiya," the man cried. "Me and the boys were just talking about you the other day. We were having a good laugh about the time you almost set the kitchen on fire trying to fill in for me. How ya been?"

"I've been better. I'm still trying to figure out this thing called life but I'm getting by day to day. How are the kids?"

"Oh they're fine. The twins are getting big and Ana is pretty busy with the new one. Say, if you need a job I could use you at the little place I am working out now. No benefits but you'll know everybody there and it's pretty easy. It's like we are getting one over on them."

Catawba took a deep breath and studied the man's wizened face as he thought about what to say.

"No thanks man. I believe I'll just mosey on down the road and see what happens."

3

"Well it was good to see you," he said as he squeezed Catawba's shoulder.

"You too."

Catawba carried his groceries outside and put them in the backseat of the car. He got in and peered out the windshield as he tapped his fingers on the steering wheel. I have to get in gear, he thought. He put his seatbelt on, cranked the car, and headed up the road to his grandfather's house.

In fifteen minutes he was there. He pulled up behind the house, fished a bag from behind his seat and got out. He carried it to the backdoor, turned the knob and went inside. He walked into the kitchen to find the old man going through the silverware drawer.

"What have you lost now Pop?"

"Hey Catawba, I can't find the can opener."

"Well," he replied as he sat the bag on the counter, "it has to be somewhere."

The old man muttered something under his breath, grabbed his walker and took off through the house. Catawba watched him go and started putting away the groceries.

When he got through he washed his hands, dried them off, and took off for the living room. He found the old man sitting on the couch rubbing his knee. He sat down in a straight backed chair and started looking around the room at all the undusted knick-knacks and family photos. After a few minutes he cleared his throat and spoke.

"When did you see the can opener last?"

"Oh I don't remember to tell you the truth but we could probably find another one in the basement or attic."

"No. Don't worry about it. I'll just buy you a new one at the dollar store."

"I just have a hard time keeping things up around here. The nurse comes by most days but it still gets away from me."

"Stop kicking yourself. That's why you have me," he said calmly. "When do you go back to see the doctor at the VA hospital?"

"You wrote it down on the calendar I think."

4

Catawba stood up and looked at the wall calendar above the lamp but found that it was from the previous year and devoid of any markings. He flipped to the cardboard backing but didn't find anything there either. He sighed and turned around.

"Do you have a new calendar put up somewhere? I need to switch this one out for you."

"Why? One is just as good as the next," the old man replied gruffly.

"I'll call about the appointment this coming Monday. I think it is sometime in the middle of next month."

He sat back down in the chair and looked at his grandfather. The old man was sitting stockstill and staring at a picture on the opposing wall. After a long time he spoke.

"How long has she been gone now?"

"Who?"

"You know who."

He let out a deep sigh and turned toward his grandson.

"A couple of years if my memory is right. You were there yourself so you should know. We spent close to sixty years right here in this house. Then one day you find yourself walking through the house or sitting on the couch and you turn to say something to her and it hits you all over again. So I sit here all day long rubbing my arthritis and thinking about days gone by. Did I ever tell you about our trip out west in the sixties?"

"No. I don't think so."

"It was in sixty-three. I remember because it was right before President Kennedy got killed. There wasn't a job to be found around here at the plants so your grandmother and me loaded up in the car with your mom and uncle. They were both tiny then. We took off and went out to South Dakota to see if I could get a rig job but there wasn't anything out there either. I left them there with one of our distant cousins and went on out through Wyoming but I couldn't find anything in that part of the country either. So I came back and got them and we headed back here. At some spot in the road close to Knoxville the car blew up. I traded it and a hundred dollars for a car that was even older but it got us back home."

5

"What did you do then?"

"I lucked up a few months later and got on with a plumbing outfit in town."

"I've never heard that story before."

"Don't worry about it. It's over now. What are you doing for a job these days?"

"Well," Catawba said slowly, "since my last dismissal nothing much. I still have some money left in the bank. So I take care of you the best I can and I try to write some. Other than that I haven't found anything worth a moment's concern. Just dead end jobs for a dead end life."

"You have to find something sooner or later. That way you don't blow through what little money you have left. You ought to apply for a summer job up there at that park next to your house, the one at the lake. You're always hiking around in it. It's close by and you haven't been fired from there yet."

"I'll think about that. It would be nice to get paid to be outside in nature and bask in the sun but I've heard they're not fond of hiring us locals. That's why I've never considered it."

"Go ahead. What's the worst that can happen at a lake?"

"Don't worry. I'll find something to do for money and maybe if I get ahead I'll go out west and take you with me. You can go yell your name into the Grand Canyon or go rock climbing in the Rockies. Hell, we can even float you and your walker down the Colorado River and..."

"Shut up Catawba," the old man said with a grin, "and stop trying to rile me up."

"Well if you're feeling better about all things big and small I'll go home now so I can put up my groceries too."

"You do that and don't forget my can opener."

"Don't worry I won't forget."

Catawba stood up and headed out of the living room. He walked through the house and went out the backdoor. He turned around on the cement steps and made sure the outer door was shut. Then he went over and got in the car and drove home.

2

After breakfast the next morning he got out the phonebook and looked up the number for the park service office. He punched in the digits and sat down in a chair at the kitchen table. A gruff secretary answered the phone and informed him that hiring for the summer season started on the last Monday of the month. He thanked him, hung up the phone, and looked over at the calendar. "Eight days away," he whispered. "I can find something else before then."

He jumped on the internet and looked up temp jobs in the area but found nothing listed except construction jobs in surrounding counties and night cleaning for government institutions. He looked at the classifieds in an old newspaper but only found the usual assortment of get-rich-quick schemes.

He picked up the phone again and called around to his acquaintances and distant family members. He found out through the genetic grapevine that his distant cousin Eustace had started a new and exciting career as the regional distributor for a large company that specialized in cleaning equipment. He thought for a minute and then called Eustace as fast as his fingers could dial. He answered after several rings and told Catawba that it was true, he had embarked on a business opportunity like no other. Then he told him to come by his house so they could discuss it further. He agreed, hung up the phone, grabbed his keys, and took off in search of El Dorado.

When he got to the house he found his cousin lying in bed and staring up at the ceiling. He stood there and looked at him in confusion.

"Umm," Catawba said slowly, "I thought you were running a business?"

Eustace whirled around to the edge of the bed and looked at his visitor.

"Now Catawba I have it all lined up. We go around and sell these vacuum cleaners door-to-door. There are at least ten thousand people right now in Fonta Flora chomping at the bit for a product like this."

"Tell me more cousin ."

"Well you just take a gander at this pamphlet here," Eustace said as he handed him a trifold brochure from off the nightstand.

Catawba grabbed it and looked at the cover. There was a family smiling and clapping as a man in a three-piece suit demonstrated a shiny canister vacuum's potential. Awesome, he thought. He opened up the brochure to find a cartoonish collage of door-to-door salesmen counting money and waving from a yacht that was overflowing with leggy blonde models. Catawba grinned like a Cheshire cat and looked up.

"I see that tickles your money spot."

"Eustace, tell me how all this works."

"Okay. We work on commission, or rather I work on commission and give you a kick back until you establish your own clientele," he said as he got out a cigarette, "but just starting out you'll go around with me and be my helper. This is the perfect job for a learned young man such as yourself."

"I don't know. This isn't some hayseed get-rich-quick scheme is it? Be honest with me and don't waste my time."

"Of course not. I used to teach Sunday school. I'm as straight as an arrow."

"Ok then, when do we start and how much do I get for a kickback?"

He snickered as he lit his cigarette. He stared at the floor for a moment and then looked up.

"First impressions with the customers are everything. Do you have dress clothes and a tie?"

"Yes cousin I do. Ready, willing, and able."

"Well you come back bright and early in the morning dressed to the hilt and we'll go get our first units. Then off we go to the houses. I'll give you a hundred dollars on every unit we sell and I'll throw in lunch."

"Deal," Catawba replied as he reached out and shook his hand.

He went back home and went to work. He pressed his good slacks and polished his penny-loafers. That night in bed he could hardly stay still or keep his eyes closed.

When the alarm clock went off he shot out of bed and took a shower. He hopped out, dried off, had a light breakfast, put on his threads, and took off for a busy day of adventure capitalism. He got to Eustace's house in no time and stood outside knocking on the door.

"It's open," shouted a groggy voice from inside.

He went inside and found his cousin still in his sleep shorts and sitting on the edge of the bed. He looked around the room at all the beer bottles and remnants of a possible chainsmoker's convention.

"Uh Eustace, are we working today?"

"Of course we are. I just need to get going," he replied as he scratched his big paunch.

"Okay, I guess. I'll give you a minute."

He went to the kitchen and made some coffee and sat down at the table. Eustace came stumbling through when it was almost done perking. He yawned and stretched and scratched his belly again before heading on to the bathroom. He came out after a while, walked past the coffee pot, and went back to his bedroom.

Catawba sat there and listened to the grunting and shuffling of feet. After a few minutes he decided to get up and go check on him. He found his cousin putting on dress clothes that didn't appear to have been washed or ironed in ages. Eustace tied his tie, lit a cigarette, kicked back on the bed, and began staring up at the ceiling as if studying on some unknown mystery. Catawba stood there waiting as he smoked away. After a few puffs he stood up and said he was ready to go.

They walked outside together and climbed into Eustace's twenty year old hatchback and took off for town like Mormon missionaries. Twenty minutes later they pulled up in front of an unmarked metal building with a couple of open garage doors.

"Stay here," Eustace said as he got out of the car.

He took off for one of the open bay doors. He tried to go in but was stopped by a bulldog looking man in a tie. Catawba could tell they were having a lively discussion by the fierce gesticulations being exchanged. After a few minutes the man allowed Eustace to go inside. He came back outside pulling a vacuum cleaner and looking defeated. He took it to the back of the car, opened the hatch, and put it in. He slammed the hatch, got back in the driver's seat, and looked at Catawba.

"That miserly old bastard said I could only take one unit since I don't have collateral," he barked out as he dug around for his cigarettes.

"So what happens when we sell the only unit?"

"Oh, we'll just come back and get another one. See Catawba this is the kind of give and take there is in the world of competitive commerce."

"I hope you're right," he replied anxiously.

He pulled the gear shift into drive and they took off for the start of the route. They went through the center of town where the rich people lived, past the suburbs where the middle class people lived, and finally out to the barren farmland in the middle of the countryside. Catawba looked around but only saw cows and abandoned clapboard houses.

"Why are we going out here to sell vacuum cleaners to these destitute souls? Shouldn't we have hit up the rich people in town?"

"Those rich people have housekeepers and servants. These people out here are shut off from stores and whatnot. They do most of their trading with people who go door-to-door. Don't worry, I've thought this through."

"Well you're the boss."

Eustace drove on to the county line and cut down a road lined with ancient mill houses. He headed toward the end of the road and parked on the shoulder close to the cul-de-sac.

"You let me do most of the talking. You just get the vacuum cleaner out, carry it in, and smile while I demonstrate," he said before hoping out.

Catawba climbed out and went to the back and opened up the faded hatch. He lugged the thing out and took off after Eustace.

"Keep it out of the dirt."

"Sorry cuz," he replied as he lassoed the hose off the grass.

Eustace went to the closest house and started knocking on the door as a cow bellowed on the hill behind the house.

The house was ghostly quiet and he shot Catawba a quick glance of apprehension. Then they heard the pitter-patter of feet inside. The door opened and a small girl with pigtails stuck her head out.

"Hey there sweetheart, my name is Eustace Fox and I am an authorized distributor for the Carolina Canister Vacuum Cleaner Company and I'm out here trying to…"

The little tyke slammed the door before he could finish. He stood there for a second looking at the door in silence. Then he turned around and walked back making a follow-me motion with his hand. They walked on to the next millhouse and Eustace knocked again. An old man in overalls came out and Eustace made his sales pitch. The old man blinked twice and went back inside and shut the door. Eustace walked back to where Catawba was standing with the cumbrous machine.

"I don't know man. Maybe it isn't the right time of the month for the relief checks to be issued. I mean, it is Monday right?"

"Dude, it is the third Monday of the month. Were you banking on some old bird parting with their social security check to buy this damn machine?"

"Now I never said that. Government money spends just like it all does. I sell equally to all people regardless of age or infirmity."

"Yeah I bet you do."

"Follow me and watch," Eustace said as he took off across the grass. "I bet this machine is about to leap out of your arms and into someone's living room."

He went up to the next door and knocked. A middle aged woman with horn-rimmed glasses came out and stared at him. Eustace sermonized and gesticulated for a moment and then motioned for Catawba to go inside.

He carried the unit through the front door and sat it down on a tattered old rug in the center of the livingroom . He bent at the waist and tried to unkink the hose as Eustace and the woman came in behind him and stood there watching. He stood up when he had everything in order and smiled.

Eustace reached down and got out the retractable cord and looked around the room for a plug in. He saw one in the corner and walked over to it. He fingered the cobwebs off the cover and plugged it in. He turned around and shuffled back and grabbed the hose. He looked at the woman and she looked back bewildered.

"Let me show you dear what you've been missing your whole life," he said as he reached down and turned the thing on.

He made a nice presentation that included engineering terms he didn't grasp and financial commitments she couldn't digest. When he had sucked all the life out of the rug he reached down and turned it off.

"Now honey, this unit right here can be yours today for nine hundred dollars cash or a thousand fifty if you finance with us and pay a hundred down," Eustace said in his most sugary sweet voice.

"Be right back. Let me get my purse," she said as she took off for the back of the house.

"Now see there Catawba , easy-peasey."

They stood there looking at each other while she rummaged around in what sounded like wooden cabinets. She came shuffling back with a little leather change purse in her hand. Eustace gave her an uneasy glance as she undid the clasp and pulled out a small wad of bills. She began sifting through her currency, her face twitching as she studied her finances.

"Let's see, I got forty-two dollars here. Unless I throw in the fifteen I was going to spend tomorrow at the church bake sale."

The veins on Eustace's head popped out and his face grew cherry red. Catawba shook his head and sighed.

"That be enough young man? How much did you say I need?"

Eustace reached down, yanked the cord out of the wall, and bear hugged the unit to his chest.

"Get the damn door for me," he said in a pained tone.

Catawba walked over and opened the door as his cousin stormed out with a death grip on the vacuum. They double timed it through the yards and headed for the car. When they got to the back bumper Eustace told him to open the hatch.

12

When he did Eustace slung the thing in, slammed the hatch, and leaned against the car. Then a voice came from the yard beside them.

"Hey there young man," a man called out as he looked at Eustace.

"Yeah, you looking for a way to improve your household cleanliness?"

"Nah, this old place is fine. I was wondering if you could maybe take me up the road to the beer store."

Eustace mumbled some profanities, got in the car, and cranked it. Catawba went over and got in too. Eustace wheeled the car around and took off cursing. He drove directly back to his house. He pulled up in the driveway, got out and went inside. Catawba sat there for a while looking around before deciding to go in and check on him. He found his cousin already in his sleep shorts, lying on the bed, and smoking a cigarette.

"Are we calling it a day?" he asked gently.

"Hell yeah, call me tomorrow. We have to come up with a better plan of attack. Oh and cut the lights off as you leave."

"Okay, I'll call you in the morning."

Eustace muttered something inaudible as Catawba turned around and went out and shut the door. He drove home in silence, stopping only to get a magazine.

After breakfast the next morning he tried calling Eustace. He called several times but no one answered. As the forenoon marched on he grabbed his keys and went back.

He banged on the front door and side door, but heard nothing except the faint whisper of a floor fan. He went back to the front door again and knocked even harder. He heard the shuffle of feet approaching the door, then a small crack appeared in the mini-blinds.

"Catawba I got some bad news for you," Eustace said groggily.

"Yeah and what's that?"

"That man from the warehouse came out yesterday and got the vacuum cleaner unit. He said we were not cut out to represent their business in any way, shape, or form. But don't worry though, I have plenty of other business ideas brewing in my head. Have you ever tried your hand at digging ginseng in the national forest?"

"You listen here fatboy," Catawba said loudly. "You said I was going to get paid for selling units. You didn't say anything about quitting as soon as we started or digging ginseng. You are at least going to give me my gas money."

"Check in the car ashtray. There's money there. Trust me."

He walked out to the car and opened the door. He pulled the ashtray out to find a small pile of discolored pennies. He snatched them up and went back to the front door. He threw them as hard as he could and yelled at the top of his lungs. He heard the lazy shuffle of feet and then silence.

"Go to the side door," Eustace called out from somewhere in the back of the house.

Catawba marched around to the side door and saw a twenty dollar bill shoot out the mail slot. He reached down and picked it up.

"You are one more clodhopper," he yelled as he walked away.

"Yeah and I ain't in the business of keeping up the entire county," Eustace yelled back.

He climbed in the car, slammed the door and left. He found the highway heading back home busy with the traffic of utility trucks, slow pokes, speed demons, and other country road driving incompetents but he shrugged it off and kept going. When he got to the lake he turned onto his road to see a disheveled and glassy-eyed man standing against the guardrail. He slowed down and pulled off onto the shoulder of the road. He looked at the man for a second and then rolled down his window.

"Are you alright? Do you need some help?"

"Yessum. I'm heading to Lenoir City," the man replied as he walked toward the car.

"That's thirty miles away. How are you going to get there?"

"My ride will be along directly."

Catawba looked out through the windshield and sighed. He thought for a second and then nudged the bottles and papers from the passenger's side seat into the floorboard. He looked back at the man and saw that he was looking off into the woods.

"Get in and I'll take you."

"Yessum."

The man walked over, opened the door, and got in. He shut the door and grabbed the window knob and cranked the handle until the glass was down. Catawba sat there watching him in silent contemplation. Then he looked in the rearview mirror and crept back onto the road.

He drove through miles of countryside and fertile bottomland before he reached the main highway that led to Lenoir City. His passenger sat there soundless with his eyes fixed on some alien point in the landscape. When they went across the old bridge at the dump he looked over at the man and then back at the road.

"Say, how did you get to that place back there where I picked you up."

"Dropped off. Hard for a man to get his bearings these days."

"Well who do you know in Lenoir City?"

"My sis and her boy. They'll be havin' supper directly."

Catawba looked down at the old clock dial on the dashboard and rolled his eyes. He kept going and didn't say anything. When they got to the city limits the man made a lazy motion with his hand. Catawba turned down a side street with row after row of rickety old apartment buildings and abandoned mobile homes.

"Up here," the man said, pointing with a thumb tip.

They pulled up in front of a three story apartment building with cracked bricks and chipping paint. Catawba looked out his window and saw a group of swarthy faced kids kicking a soccer ball back and forth beneath a pine tree. The man didn't say anything as he got out and stood scratching his chest.

After a minute he took off in a fast trot. He went past the kids and headed towards the building. He went up the stairwell to the second floor and stopped at the third door. Catawba watched as the man started banging away on the door with all his might. The door flung open and a bald headed

15

man stepped outside. The man made a few quick hand motions, shook his head, and went back inside. The hitchhiker stood there for a second before turning around and coming back towards the car. He climbed back in the passenger's side seat and looked at Catawba.

"That man didn't speak rightly good English. I'm not sure but I'm guessin ' they moved."

"Well do you have someplace else to go?"

"It'll be alright."

Catawba sat there rubbing his forehead and thinking as the man started digging around in the floorboard. He came up with a pop bottle that had a few drops of sludge in the bottom. He went to twist the top off but Catawba looked at him and shook his head. The man stopped with his mouth ajar.

"Look, I'll buy you a pack of crackers and a can drink at the store. Then I'll take you to the men's shelter back in town."

"That'll do. Thank y a."

Catawba cranked the car, circled around and took off. After they had gone a few miles he looked over at his passenger.

"Did he say how long ago they moved?"

"Nah. He said something about how he'd been livin' there for ten years."

"And when was the last time you saw your sister?"

"We all worked together at the plant years ago when Reagan was in office."

"My god man, do you have any idea what year it is?"

"Yessum," the man replied with indifference.

Catawba refocused on the road and picked up speed. He stopped at the gas station on the outskirts of the city and told the man to sit still while he went in. He got out and looked around at the hot and hazy parking lot but there was nothing and nobody. He went into the store and came back out with a paper poke for the man and a six pack of beer for himself. He got in, put the beer on the floorboard, and handed the poke to the man. He watched as he started rooting around in it. He brought out an off-brand cola and a pack of peanuts and attacked them with a ravenous fury.

They drove on into town and got on the bypass. They zoomed through several lights and then cut off and went down an alley lined with neglected bushes. They bounced across the gravel until they got to the men's shelter at the end of the road. The derelict building was devoid of any markings except for a small cross painted on the door. The man pitched his trash back into the bag and got out.

"Hey," Catawba said as he looked at the man through the open window, "do you have a name?"

"Yessum. My name is Norton."

Norton looked at Catawba and back at the building. He took off walking towards the door, slicking his hair back as he went. He got to the door and started knocking. Catawba went to crank the car but stopped when he saw Norton pacing back and forth peeping in the front windows of the shelter. He sat there for a minute watching the scene. Then he got out and walked over to him.

"I don't think they're open yet," Norton said.

"Let me look."

Catawba walked up to the door and read the sign. Then walked back to where Norton was standing and stopped.

"The sign says they don't admit people before seven. That's hours away. Do you have anyone you can call?"

"Why yes I do. I can call my brother. He lives on the mountaintop at the other end of the county."

"Well Norton, you'll have to ride with me to my house. I don't have a cellphone."

They went back to the vehicle and got in and left. He drove directly to his house and got out. He grabbed his beer and motioned for Norton to get out too. They went up on the porch and Catawba sat the beer down against a column. He told Norton to have a seat while he went inside to get the phone. Norton sat down and Catawba disappeared through the door.

He came back out with the phone and handed it to Norton. Catawba stood there as he dialed in a number and started talking. He listened half-heartedly at first but grew more attentive when Norton started yelling random words into the phone. Then he clicked the phone off and handed it back to Catawba.

"He'll be by directly. Say, could you spare one of those cold beers?"

"I will give you one and only one and then someone needs to show up for you," Catawba said sternly.

"That'll do."

Catawba reached down and passed him a bottle of beer. He stood there watching as Norton uncapped the bottle and commenced sucking at it with all his might. He finished it in a flash and wiped his mouth with the back of his hand. He sat the empty bottle down and looked up at his benefactor with a smile. Catawba sighed and carried the phone back inside the house. He hung it up and fed the cat and got a glass out of the cabinet. He walked back out on the porch to find that Norton and his beer had disappeared. His face turned cherry red as he took off running down the front steps and into the yard. He looked around but didn't see anything. He heard the sound of far off laughter and sprinted to the back of the house. He looked out across his neighbor's cow pasture to see Norton carrying the beer and bolting for the woods.

Catawba took off after him but stopped when he saw him disappear into a stand of pine trees. That's par for my life, he thought. He turned around and went back inside the house and didn't stir for the rest of the day.

3

A few days later he opened the backdoor of his grandfather's house and went inside. He sat the new can opener down on the kitchen table and looked around. The old man had been baking or so it seemed because the sink was full of dirty dishes and pans. He walked into the living room and found his grandfather sitting on the couch and tinkering in the back of the cuckoo clock.

"What are you doing? You don't know anything about cogs and gear," he said before sitting down.

"Hey Catawba, this thing just doesn't swing," he replied.

"Swing? Do you mean the pendulum on the front?"

"Yeah. Yeah. The pendulum."

"Let me look," he said as he got up.

He walked over and eased the clock up from the couch cushion. He flipped it over and saw that the pendulum was gone. He handed it back and glanced around the room.

"When was the last time you heard that thing ticking?"

"It always ticks. This clock is sixty years old and keeps time with the best of them."

"I hope you can fix it because I don't know anything about cuckoos."

"Don't worry," he said as he put it up to his ear and shook it, "it has to be something simple."

He walked back over and sat down in the chair. His grandfather studied the arcana of the clock until he lost interest, then he sat it aside and sighed.

"Hey Pop, remember the other day when you said I ought to get a job with the park service up there next to my house?"

"Yeah?"

"I think I am going to do it. A government job like that would suit me just fine. Fresh air and sunshine."

"Catawba, did something happen that you're not telling me about?"

"What do you mean?"

"Nothing. I guess."

"Don't worry, it's nothing bad. I just don't think the private sector is as reliable in this day and age."

"I wouldn't know. I don't get out much. I just watch the news and the world is going to hell. Things must be pretty bad with all the scam phone calls I get. Every one of them is looking to pilfer me out of a nickel."

"I bet."

"They keep talking about porch pirates on the TV too. I hope they don't rob me blind."

"I don't think you have anything those people want. Look, I called the VA hospital and you don't go back to see the doctor until the end of next month."

"They wouldn't know. Our entire government is a bunch of crooks. I wouldn't trust any of those people."

"Gee, you just told me a few days ago to go get a job with the park service."

"Now, I didn't mean for it to be a career. It's just until you get your bearings in the encyclopedia world."

"Encyclopedias?"

"Yeah, you wanted to sell encyclopedias or write them didn't you?"

"I want to write books, not encyclopedias."

"Why would anyone read a book when they have a good TV set?"

"Pop, why would anyone read an encyclopedia when there's the internet?"

"Catawba, I still look things up in the encyclopedia," the old man replied sternly.

"Yeah and I still read books."

"That's because you're destitute. I bet with your first paycheck you go out and buy a nice wood paneled floor model TV from Sears and Roebuck."

"Say what? They haven't made those things in forty years."

"That's the reason I need to be on the lookout for porch pirates."

"Are you messing with me?"

"No," he replied with a grin. "Why would I do that?"

"I don't know. Anyway, going back, way back, the park service job would only be for the busy season."

"That's good. Then you can go back to school."

"Oh no, I'm not going back. I'm not paying a king's ransom when I can go to the public library for free."

"Shit Catawba, back in the sixties when I got my plumber's license from the state the fee wasn't even twenty dollars."

Catawba laughed as he stood up and walked over to the couch. He picked up the cuckoo clock and carried it over to the wall and rehung it. He turned around and walked back to the couch.

"Pop, I'm not going back to the university. I can't stand to be around those wallflowers. Besides, who is going to take care of you if I leave?"

20

"Now I didn't mean it like that. I meant you could take a personal enrichment course right here at the junior college. Look."

The old man leaned forward to the coffee table, got the newspaper, and offered it to him. Catawba grabbed it, walked over to the chair, sat down and unfolded it. He read the front page of the Fonta Flora Gazette and then looked over at his grandfather.

"Well let's see here, they found a meth lab and busted a dozen people for stealing scrap metal. There was an arson and a mental patient is on the loose. Oh, and let's not forget the new artisanal coffee house. That's quite the concoction there. And what kind of personal enrichment skills do you see me getting around here? Barista at the state penitentiary?"

"No. Flip to the back page," the old man said without humor.

He flipped to the backpage and read the offerings from the junior college. Then he looked back at his grandfather.

"I don't see anything enriching."

"Look at the English classes offered."

"There's only one listed. I'm not quite sure what the class is about but I'm not paying for it."

"I'll pay for it. No matter what the cost. Just so I can show you that things are not that expensive in this world."

"And the textbook too . Don't be an old tightwad."

"That's a deal. Tomorrow is Friday. You can come pick me up and I'll wait in the car while you register. I want to get out of the house for a while."

"That's fine. I'll come early in the morning. I want to beat the heat and I have a few things to attend to at the house later on. I think they probably open up at about eight or nine."

"Okay."

Catawba stood up and went to say goodbye but stopped when the old man grabbed the TV remote. The TV flashed on and he sighed. He walked out of the house and to his car and left for home.

He stopped at the end of his driveway, got the mail, and drove on up to the house. He went inside and made lunch and ate in quietude as the cat caught forty winks beside the hearth.

That afternoon he was sitting at his desk staring at the keyboard when he heard knocking on the front door. Bam. Bam. Bam. He jumped up and went to the front door. He flung it open to find a silver haired man standing there in a farmer's outfit.

"Hello Catawba, I'm your distant cousin. My name is Brady," the man said as he extended his hand.

"Ok," he replied as he shook.

"Yeah I stopped by here because I wanted to know about the cellphone tower on the hill behind your house."

"It's not mine. It's the neighbor's."

"Can we go look at it?"

"Sure Brady," he replied as he headed for the porch steps.

They walked to the back of the house and got on the service road. Catawba gritted his teeth as he began walking with his bare feet on the loose gravel rocks. He stopped when he got to the top of the ridge and looked around. Then he walked over to the metal fence and undid the gate clasp as Brady stood wheezing beside him.

"Are you alright man?"

"Yeah, I'm just a little bit older than you are. That hill was a monster."

"I guess we can go inside. Just take pictures with your phone quickly."

He followed him through the gate and to the wooden fence that marked the security perimeter of the cell tower. Brady pulled out his phone and started snapping away at the business placards and warning signs.

Then he stopped and looked over at Catawba. Catawba nodded and took off walking back through the gate with Brady in tow. He closed the gate and refastened the latch.

"Got it?"

"Yeah, I got it," he said, still breathing heavily, "I want to have a tower put up on mom's property above the farm."

"Well I think the phone company pays good money to lease land like this but I don't know to tell you the truth."

"That's what I thought too."

He fished a business card out of the bib pocket of his overalls and passed it over to Catawba. He held it up and read it and then placed it in his pocket. He looked over at Brady in confusion.

"It says musical savant. Mom always said you were an engineer. Or is that your brother Daniel?"

"Oh, we're both engineers. We both moved away from this state decades ago but I came back here to live after I retired. Now I play music for fun. I can play seven different instruments. What do you do?"

"I'm a jack of all trades and master of none. I like writing but I'm not mechanically or musically inclined whatsoever."

Catawba started walking back down the hill slowly with his cousin on his hip. When they got back to the driveway they stopped and looked out at the blooming wisteria that hung off the pine trees.

"This is a nice place you have here."

"Yeah, I wanted it to get the house remodeled years ago but they wouldn't touch it because of asbestos."

"Let me tell you why..."

He took a deep breath and delivered a lengthy oral essay on the chemical properties of asbestos and why the disturbance of such a substance could lead to a toxic exposure of cancer causing particles. He went on to elucidate how in his younger days as an engineer he had read up on the usage of asbestos as a heat shield in certain industrial applications and how that science still held true but otherwise better chemical compounds had been formulated by people in the private sector working in accordance with government specifications.

"And that's why your house is a deathtrap," he said in closing.

"Gee, that was uplifting."

"I'm sorry. I can get a little carried away. So how is your grandfather? I haven't seen him in years."

"The best that can be expected for a man of his age. I moved in with him for a short spell after he broke his hip but that didn't last long. We would sit around all day and argue."

23

"Why did you argue?"

"Because we're so much alike. To tell you the truth he is the only reason why I still live around here."

"Oh."

"So now I try to go over and see him every chance I get. I try to do the best I can for him but some days I find myself making excuses so I can get out of it."

"Why would you avoid going to see him?"

"Because sometimes I look at the deep lines in his face and think about how they were fed by the tributaries of time and toil and it paints a picture of human frailty. And I don't ever want to look at that picture because I know I am seeing my own future self and what man is ready to march out and meet his own mortality?"

"I hope you write stuff like that down. That's beautiful."

"Huh?"

"Go write that down and don't wait. I'll see you again," he said as he opened his car door and got in.

He shut the door and back down the driveway and headed off up the road as Catawba stood there watching him leave. Then he walked up on the porch, went inside, and headed for his desk.

4

The next morning he got up and put his clothes on and ate breakfast. He drove over to his grandfather's house and pulled up in the driveway. The old man was sitting on the porch peering out at his chickweed choked yard. He stepped out of the car and started walking towards the porch.

"Hey Pop, are you ready to go?"

"No, I've got the gas you need," the old man replied.

"Gas? We're going to town. You said you were going to pay for that summer class you told me I should take."

"You're not here to mow the grass?"

"I will when we get back, but for now, please start getting ready. I want to get down there and get back before the traffic gets heavy on the road."

"Let me close up the curtains and lock the backdoor if we're leaving," the old man said as he stood up.

24

"Cinch up your suspenders before you fall."

"If you say so Catawba."

He tightened his suspender straps and opened the screen door and went inside. Catawba followed behind him and stood in the living room looking at the coffee table. The cuckoo clock was disassembled and spread out on a hand towel. When he heard the walker coming back through the house he went back out onto the porch and stood. The old man opened the front door and stepped out. He pulled the door closed and looked at his grandson.

"Did you ever get your cuckoo clock working right?"

"I think the thing just needs a little oil on its gears."

"If you say so, Pop."

They took off down the front steps with Catawba holding onto his grandfather's shoulder for safety. They went over to the car and Catawba put the walker in the backseat while his grandfather got in.

"Put your seatbelt on," Catawba said as he closed his door.

"Alright."

He cranked the car and backed down the driveway. They took the interstate down to the junior college exit and got off. When they stopped at the traffic light he looked over at his grandfather and back at the road. The light changed and he cut onto the road and drove over to the college entrance and turned off and started a slow descent to the parking lot. The school was dead except for a small deputation of men cutting the patchy grass next to the buildings. He parked the car under an ancient and gnarled Magnolia tree and got out.

"You wait here. I'll go sign up and pay. You can just repay me."

"That'll do."

He got out and went up the cement walkway to the administration building. When he opened the glass door he was met by a wall of cold air. He went inside and stood there looking around at the various college functionaries.

"How can I help you sir?" asked a man at a desk.

"Uh yes," he replied as he walked toward the desk, "I want to sign up for a summer class."

"Here. Fill these out."

He took the clipboard and pen and carried them over to a row of folding chairs. He looked at the forms and sat down. He filled them out the best he could but he didn't know the exact date for every little particular. He signed his name and returned them to the desk. The man looked over the forms and directed him to an office where another person was typing away at a computer.

"Take a seat there sir. I'm one of the deans here at the junior college."

"Okay."

Catawba sat down and the dean started going over the forms. He stopped every so often to check the dates and signatures. He looked up after the last page and cleared his throat.

"Why do you want to take this class?"

"I don't know. I guess I'm wanting to stay current in my knowledge of all things literary."

"It says here that you've started and stopped college several times over the course of your adult life. Why is that?"

"I get tired of waiting so I leave."

"I don't understand. What are you waiting for at a college ?"

"Waiting for someone to say something profound."

"Mr. Fox, that's not the point of schools. Education is meant to help you function in an ever changing society."

"If you say so sir."

"Here you go," he said as he held out a small slip of paper. "Take this card up to the business window and pay. Then go over to the bookstore in the next building and pick up your textbook."

"Thank you."

He took the slip of paper and went over to the business desk and paid. Then he walked out of the building and headed on to the next one. He went into the bookstore and asked the worker for the required textbook. He paid, picked up the textbook, and walked back outside to his car. His grandfather was watching a worker rake up grass clippings beside the car and didn't hear him walk up. He opened the door and got in

26

and handed him the receipts and textbook. The old man bent over and began inspecting the receipts. Then he looked up at his grandson with a frown on his face.

"What kind of nonsense is this? What did you sign up for?"

"A class. Just one class. Just one summer class," he replied as he started to back out.

"My god I don't know if I can handle paying this back to you. I'm on a fixed income."

"Don't worry about paying me back. Just let this be a lesson to you that things are not what they used to be in this world."

"When does this class take up?"

"It's every Wednesday and it starts next week. This Monday is Memorial day and I have to go apply with the park service," he said as he cut onto the main highway.

"Catawba, are you still going to mow the grass for me this summer? You said that you would ."

"I'll do the best I can. Human decency takes precedence over everything else."

"Okay then."

He sped up the interstate to their exit ramp. He got off and drove back to his grandfather's house. He pulled up next to the sidewalk and opened his door and walked around and helped his grandfather get out. He handed him his walker and followed behind him as he shuffled toward the porch. Then he went back, shut the car doors, and went down to the shed.

He got the mower out and filled it with gas. He climbed on and started making passes through the weed choked yard. The mower bogged down a time or two in the thick dew that still coated the shady spots. As he started for the side yard he looked toward the porch. His grandfather was leaning against the porch column and pointing towards the road. He drove over to the porch and cut the mower off.

"What is it?"

"Knock down the bushes at the road."

"The rose bushes? Why?"

"I get sick of seeing them. I can't see traffic."

"Please go sit down."

27

He didn't take the time to see if he went back to his chair or not. He just cranked the mower and went back to work.

He finished up as the church bells near the house rang out for noon. He closed the shed door and wiped the grass clippings from his shoes. He walked back to the porch but his grandfather wasn't there. He went inside and found him in the kitchen eating fish sticks and drinking water.

"Help yourself. There's plenty here."

"I think I'll pass."

"Well be like that then."

He sat down and watched the old man masticate with fury. When he finished he took his little plate to the sink and rinsed it out. He turned around and looked at his grandson.

"Well good luck with the job Monday. I'm going to go take a nap. And here, take this."

The old man fished a five dollar bill out of his breast pocket and handed it to his grandson. He looked at it for a minute and then shoved it down inside his front pocket.

"Very generous of you. Hey, I'm going to camp out tomorrow night. I'll stop by tomorrow but I'll call you on Sunday."

The last part fell on deaf ears because the old man was already on his way to the bedroom. Catawba sighed and went outside and headed home.

When he walked through the door the cat came running up to him. He petted him and fed him and went to his bedroom closet and dug out his cantaloupe colored rucksack and camping gear. He put a small tarpaulin in the bottom and placed his ultralight sleeping bag on top of it. He finished off his pack with a flashlight and sleeve of crackers. He carried the rucksack to the backdoor and sat it down against the wall. As he turned to go back into the kitchen he heard loud knocking coming from the front door. Whack. Whack. Whack. He walked to the door and opened it up to see a bald headed man standing there rubbing his sweat covered forehead.

"Yes?"

"My name is Don and I'm your new neighbor," the man said with a smile.

"Well nice to meetcha Don. My name is Catawba. Which house did you buy?"

"I didn't buy a house. I bought the lot next to yours."

Catawba looked at the briar patch beside his driveway. He studied it for a minute and looked back at Don.

"Who are you going to get to build your house?"

"I'm going to build it myself as soon as they deliver the log cabin kit I bought out of a catalog. But for the meantime I'm going to live in an RV I found in the newspaper."

"What are you going to do about all those wild blackberry bushes and cedar trees that currently inhabit your lot?"

"I got a sling blade in the car and my girlfriend has a pair of hand clippers."

He scratched his jaw and walked over to the edge of the porch. He looked at the end of the driveway and saw an antique Mercedes convertible sitting there idling.

"That's Janice in the passenger's seat," Don said.

Catawba waved to her and she waved back. Then he turned back to Don.

"Do you guys have any clue how long it takes to clear land? I mean just to trim out a spot for an RV?"

"Don't let our age fool you. We may be retirees but we're as stout as mules."

"I'm sorry Don and where is it that you hail from?"

"We're both from Florida but we fell in love with this area years ago on our honeymoon. And we decided that when I retired from the state troopers we would relocate here."

" That's great man. Maybe with hard work and dedication you can rid this area of bandits and thievery."

"Uh, I guess I can do that for the neighborhood. And what is it that you do?"

"Um, let's see, I'm a college student and future park ranger, although the ranger part is not set in stone yet."

"Well we all have to start somewhere. I remember when I first got out of the police academy down in Tallahassee..."

"Well it was nice to meet you Don," Catawba said loudly.

He walked back inside the house and closed the door. He exhaled and took off walking to the kitchen but stopped

29

when he heard knocking again. He walked back to the door and yanked it open and looked at Don.

"What?"

"Hold on, I got you a gift basket."

Don ambled off the porch and toward the Mercedes. He reached into the backseat and brought out a dime-store wicker basket. He said something to Janice but Catawba couldn't make it out. He came back up on the porch and handed the gift basket to him. Catawba thanked him and went back inside the house. He carried the basket to the kitchen table and sat it down. He looked through it and found that it contained a few pieces of petrified fruit, an old picture book about horses, and a pair of junk store grilling tongs. He inspected the items for a minute before shoving it all back inside the basket and taking it to the trashcan and dropping it in. He shook his head as he walked through the house to his desk and sat down.

After supper he looked out the side window to check on the progress of his new neighbors. They had done nothing remarkable and stood by the car passing a joint back and forth. He cracked the window and smelled the air as he stood there watching them.

As the sunlight started to fade Don and Janice loaded up in their car and took off for parts unknown.

5

He was awakened the next morning by the groaning of a diesel engine. He sat up on the edge of the bed, wiped the sleep from his eyes, and walked to the window. Don was driving a massive bulldozer back and forth across the lot while Janice sat in a tripod camping chair watching the action. He headed to the kitchen and drank a glass of water as the noise from outside engulfed the house. Then he went back to his bedroom, put on his clothes and shoes, grabbed his keys and left.

He drove to town in a silent fury, passing cars and speeding along the way. He pulled into the farmers market but the place was empty of patrons. He got out and walked down to the cheese booth.

"Where is everyone today?"

"They're up on the hill a few streets over. They're demolishing part of the old farm and feed store."

"That's horrible. What are they doing that for? That place was a staple in this town for at least a hundred years."

"Who knows with all these out of state people moving in here," the farmer replied morosely.

"I know. I see it with my own eyes more and more."

"Let's just not talk about it anymore. So what do you want today Catawba?"

"I want some fig and honey chevre this time if you have any."

"Sure," he replied as he got out a paper poke.

Catawba paid the farmer and walked back to his car carrying his purchase. He got in and drove one street over and parked at a used car lot. He got out and headed toward the old farm store but stopped when he came upon a restless throng of people. They were standing behind a barricade watching as a group of men carried stuff outside to a dumpster. He studied the faces of the workers but couldn't identify anyone he knew so he tapped the shoulder of the man standing in front of him.

"Hey, what are they doing to the old farm store?"

"I don't know for sure but some weird acting guy with a manbun came down here and passed out these handbills."

"Well what do they say?"

"Here take mine."

"Thanks."

He took it and flipped it over and read: ChiChi Fitness Center and Kombucha Bar coming soon! He cussed as he wadded it up and pitched it into a storm drain. Then he took off walking slowly back to where he had parked.

A little while later he pulled up behind his grandfather's house. He got out and went inside and walked to the living room. He found the old man reclining on the couch and watching a Western on the TV. He stood there and waited for him to say something but he didn't. He shook his head and walked back out to his car and left. When he got home he saw that the bulldozer was gone and the lot was devoid of anything that resembled plant life.

He went inside the house and put the tub of chevre in his rucksack. He filled his canteen up with sink water and put it in the top pouch. He changed his shoes and socks and fed the cat. Then yanked up the rucksack, put it on his back, and walked out the screen door. He double timed it over to the cellphone tower service road and started climbing the hill. He stumbled a time or two on the big gravel rocks but he kept his speed up until he was on top of the ridge overlooking the lake.

He stopped and stood there watching as countless boats and one lone sloop tried to navigate the busy waters. After a few minutes he turned around and walked out to where the yellow pines started to appear. He weaved his way through the trees and used the limbs as handholds as he started his descent down the steep grade of the hill.

When he got to the flat and shady bottom he stopped amid a thicket of sassafras and studied a rivulet. The water was clear and cool to the touch. He lifted a rock and saw a long-tailed salamander wiggling about. He looked at the creature for a minute before easing the rock back down and heading on.

He made a short ascent and came out on a power company service road that was poorly maintained and choked with bramble and downed trees. He hiked out the road until he came upon the high-voltage power lines that went on in a straight line as far as the eye could see. He looked down at the sleepy and sluggish river below and smiled and started a slow descent on the kudzu covered hill. When he reached the bottom he stopped amongst some yucca bushes and looked out at the river. A great blue heron waded slowly through the water near the far shore as it hunted with deadly precision. Then he adjusted his rucksack and headed on up the river towards the bridge.

He found his normal campsite beside a gnarled river birch and poured everything out of his pack. He spread the tarp on the ground and made a cushion out of the sleeping bag. He made a snack of chevre and crackers as he sat there listening to the calls of a pileated woodpecker that was a hundred yards away. When he finished eating he dusted away the crumbs and put his back on the sleeping bag and studied the cumulus clouds that decorated the deep blue sky. Then he took a deep breath, closed his eyes, and went to sleep.

He awoke to find that the sun had set and the woods stood silent. He got up to go procure firewood but stopped when he noticed a trio of deer watching him. He stood stockstill watching as they nibbled on the scant foliage of the forest. Then they dashed off into the night and he went on. He searched around on the ground until he had an armload of firewood. He came back to the campsite and set it down. He dug out a small hole with his hands, raked up a handful of leaves, and assembled the combustibles into a teepee. He got the lighter out of a tiny pouch on his pack and flicked it several times. The dry splinters caught and the fire came to life. Then he sat back and watched as the small flames cavorted in the quietude that surrounded him.

As the fire began to die down he got up to situate his sleeping bag. He started to climb in but stopped when he heard the muffled sounds of feet and the crunching of leaves. He grabbed his flashlight, jumped up, and dashed away into the darkness from the approaching intruder.

A ruddy-faced man in a park ranger uniform came walking into the light of the fire. He stopped when he got close to the flames and stood there looking down at the fire and nudging the rucksack with the toe of his boot. Catawba took two steps forward and turned on the flashlight. The ranger didn't bother to jump, instead he just turned around and looked at him.

"No camping or fires are allowed in unauthorized areas of the park," the ranger said.

"And why is that?"

"Park service regulations. Hey, what's your name? I see you traipsing around the lake all the time."

"Catawba Fox."

"Didn't your parents give you a normal name?"

"Yes they did, but I like the ring of this name better. Besides, like a fox I can see what's happening in the dark."

"Well Catawba just don't burn the woods down. It's a holiday weekend and I have to get back to the office and all those people."

"Okay, but what's your name?"

"I'm Lowell. Ranger Lowell," the man said as he started to go.

"I'm applying Monday for a job with y'all."

Ranger Lowell turned around and stared at him. Catawba realized his error and turned the flashlight off.

"You're a little late to the party but we always need people for the busy season. No one wants to work for the park service anymore because picking up trash and babysitting the general public is something that most people find disgusting. I'll tell them at the office you're coming by Monday morning. We have to work every weekend just so you know."

"That's fine. I don't mind that at all."

"Okay," Lowell said as he turned around and left.

Catawba sat back down on the tarp and had a drink of water from his canteen. He heard the footsteps retreating but then they stopped abruptly.

"Hey," Lowell yelled out from somewhere in the dark forest.

"Yeah," he yelled back.

"If you can see in the dark then why do you need a flashlight?"

"So I can signal for help if my camp is overrun by the government's red- headed stepchildren," he shouted at the top of his lungs.

He climbed into his sleeping bag laughing at the ranger's profanity as it echoed through the darkness. He worked his body around until he was comfortable and laid there looking up at the slow movement of the heavenly bodies until his eyes grew heavy and he went to sleep.

He woke up before dawn and sat there listening to the nightbirds as they issued their final calls. When the morning light started to creep through the trees he packed up his stuff and headed on for the bridge at the other end of the forest. He got there just as the bright sunshine started to paint the tops of the white pine trees. He scurried up the embankment, climbed over the guardrail, and began walking up the road towards home.

34

When he got within eyeshot of his driveway he saw a small third-handed RV sitting on the freshly graded dirt but didn't see the Mercedes. He walked on and went inside his house. He tossed the rucksack down in a corner, fed the cat, and walked back outside. He walked slowly toward the RV, studying everything as he went. The hunk of junk was sitting on cinder blocks and the door was secured by a piece of rusty bailing twine. He grinned and went back to his house.

In the afternoon he took a shower and called his grandfather. The old man said he was fine and that he had slept well. He hung up the phone and went to his bookshelf. He looked at the various tomes and decided on his old tattered copy about a certain desperate day for the debauched denizens of Dublin. He sat down at his desk and read for the rest of the daylight hours.

6

He woke up bright and early Monday morning and got ready. He brushed his teeth and combed his hair and put his clothes on. He walked outside to see Janice unloading pots of fugly flowers from the trunk of the Mercedes. He gave her a half hearted wave as he opened the car door and climbed in. He shut the door and backed down the driveway to the road and took off. When he got to the park it was already full with people scurrying back and forth carrying their picnic supplies. He threaded his way through the visitors and parked in the overflow lot. Then he got out and headed for the park office.

He opened the office door to find a handful of disgruntled funseekers heckling a short statured park ranger. He stepped inside and stood by a stuffed bobcat until they were all gone. Then he walked up to the frazzled ranger behind the plexiglass.

"I'm Catawba."

"Okay," the ranger replied hesitantly, "and just what do you want me to do about it?"

"Ranger Lowell was supposed to tell you guys that I was coming by to apply for a job today."

"Oh yes, here," the ranger said as he ducked under the counter, "fill out an application,"

He stood up and handed him an application and a pen. Catawba took it and went back outside. He went to the only empty picnic table he could find and sat down and started filling out the application. He wrote down the usual redundant unnecessaries and signed his name. Then he stood up and took the application back. The ranger was again swamped by a deluge of people asking questions. He put the application on the counter and the ranger held up his forefinger. When the people filed out the ranger told him to meet him outside at the basement door in thirty minutes. Catawba turned around and went back out.

He went back through the picnic area again, this time looking at the roaring grills and the big families standing around licking their chops. He walked on and came to a sandy point next to the swimming area. He leaned up against the parapet and took in the scene. The kids yelled out and splashed each other, the old men laid around telling salacious jokes, and the women sunbathed as the cries of their diapered offspring fell upon deaf ears. He turned to walk back but stopped when a chubby boy in swim trunks came running up to him.

"Hey mister, want to see a magic trick?"

"Uh, sure, I guess."

The kid gave him the finger and sprinted off into the picnic area shrieking with laughter. Catawba's face flushed red and his blood pressure shot up. He took a few angered steps but then he stopped and burst out in laughter too. He smiled as he headed back up the little hill toward the office.

He knocked on the door of the basement and waited. The ranger opened it and motioned him into a small musky room with tables and taxidermied animals and two chairs under a fluorescent light. He sat down in the first chair and the ranger seated himself in the opposite chair. The ranger studied the application for a few minutes and then looked up.

"Catawba Fox, My name is Ranger Ed Lansing and I'm over all the seasonal personnel," he said with a pronounced Midwestern accent.

"Nice to meet you sir. I see you sometimes when I am out walking but I didn't know your name."

36

"Yes, that's me. First off, let me ask you, why do you want to work here at Lake Linville Park?"

"Well sir," Catawba started slowly, "As an avid consumer of the many recreational activities offered by this majestic institution I feel the need to return the favor and contribute to the upkeep of our local ecology. Furthermore, since I am a lifelong resident of the area I think I can assist the park in establishing strong community ties which will be a recipe for success for future generations of park visitors."

"Well I see you're full of shit," he said with a twinge of amusement. "Just be honest, you live nearby and you need a summer job."

"Yes sir."

"Says here on your application that you have never worked at any job for longer than six months. Why is that?"

"There's not too many jobs for the habitual daydreamer,"

"That's true but you're almost thirty."

"I know. I know. But I'm just sort of here. I exist."

"I can clearly see that. It doesn't take a rocket scientist to babysit the general public. Just someone who shows up."

"I would agree and I can do that."

Lansing nodded and looked down at the application and made a few quick marks with a pen. Then he looked up again.

"You'll work the three day weekend, Friday through Sunday. You'll start at seven in the morning and work until four. You just report here to the office this coming Friday morning and wait. The other four days of the week you can go pick blueberries or skip rocks or whatever it is you do in the woods by yourself all the time."

"Okay but what am I supposed to do all day?"

"Excuse me?"

"I mean do I go stand in the picnic area or..."

"No. You'll be supervised by me but you'll be attached to Vance. He is a lifelong seasonal employee who has done everything in the park service there is to do except be a ranger."

"Why hasn't he been a ranger?"

"How in the hell am I supposed to know that? He's a very high energy person for someone his age. You just listen to him and me and you'll do fine. Sometimes you may have to assist the maintenance man with various trail projects. His name is Lenny."

"What does Ranger Lowell do? I met him the other night."

"He patrols the boundaries to stop illegal camping. Now there is another ranger named John Quincy. He is our resident biologist and ornithologist. He is a very low key person. He probably won't talk to you."

"Okay."

"Do you have any questions?"

"Who is over the park?"

"That would be the superintendent. His name is Mooseberg. I would let you meet him but he is away right now attending a leadership summit. You won't see him anyway unless you screw something up or someone from the media shows up with a camera."

"Anything special I need to look out for?"

"I'll give you a short list of the rules and regulations that govern the park system and I'll give you some official t-shirts to wear. Just look out for children and senior citizens. Every senior citizen is a damn anarchist on some level. Make sure no one consumes any alcoholic beverages and you cannot accept any gifts from visitors. We really frown on lazy employees who just want to go hide out in the picnic area and eat with the visitors."

"I think I got it sir."

"Good," he replied as he stood up.

Him and Lansing shook hands with a smile and then walked out of the basement together. Catawba followed him up the wooden steps and stood outside the backdoor while he went in. He zoned out as he watched the hordes of people going past on their way to the beach for a day of lakeside merrymaking. He felt a smack on his shoulder and turned around to see Lansing holding out shirts and a piece of paper. Catawba grabbed the items, gave him a valedictory nod, and headed for his car.

When he pulled up in his driveway he saw that his new neighbors had hung a million different flags from the roof of their discolored sheet metal domicile. He got out and tried to study the flags and their meanings but nothing came to mind.

He grabbed his park stuff and textbook and went inside his house. He tossed the shirts in a chair and went to his desk and sat down. He read a third of the park service rules and regulations but quickly lost interest in the bureaucratic gobbledygook and sat it aside. He opened the English textbook and started fingering through the first chapter but found the content tedious so he sat it aside too. He got up and walked to his bed and kicked off his shoes and laid down. Then he sighed as he looked up at the ceiling.

7

The next day he went over to his grandfather's house. When he walked through the backdoor he met a wall of hellishly hot air. He went to the table and sat down as the old man stood at the stove forking fish sticks into a plastic bowl.

When he finished his task he took the bowl over and put it in the refrigerator. He walked back to the sink and got a cup of water and chugged it. Then he wiped his mouth with the back of his hand and stood there looking at his grandson.

"What?"

"Pop it's almost June. Don't you think we need to turn on the AC?"

"Nonsense. That'd freeze me to death. Remember the doctor said I have poor circulation and don't forget I'm on a fixed income. I don't have the money to cool you and me and every damn person in the county. Besides I saw on the..."

"Okay. Okay. You've made your point."

The old man frowned. He sat the cup down and shuffled to the table and pulled out a chair. He sat down and looked over at his grandson.

"Hey Pop guess what?"

"What?"

"I got that job with the park service."

"I knew you would," the old man said proudly. "They'd be honored to have someone of your caliber."

"Can I ask you a question?"

"Sure."

"Pop, are you an anarchist?"

"Lord no, I was a volunteer firefighter for a few years back in the late sixties and early seventies. Why do you ask?"

"At the interview the ranger said all senior citizens are anarchists. What do you think he meant by that?"

"I'm not sure, but I think he knows that most of us older people have lived long enough to see through their nonsense."

"That makes sense I guess. Hey, I was in town the other day and they are turning the old farm and feed store into a fitness center and kombucha bar."

"What's kumucha?"

"It's a health elixir they make out of mushrooms but I've never had any."

"That sounds disgusting. What happened to people drinking water?"

"I don't know but it must be a fad."

"Well," the old man said as he stood up, "it's their money."

He shuffled out the door as Catawba sat there looking at his grandmother's tureen on the shelf. He got up and walked over to it. He lifted the lid to look inside but sat it back down quickly when he heard his grandfather coming back through the house. He went back to the table and sat down as his grandfather came ambling back through the door. He stopped at the head of the table and leaned on the chair and looked at his grandson.

"Hey Pop, I forgot to tell you this but they sold that lot next to my house. A couple of weird retirees from Florida bought it. They said they are going to build a house."

"I never did see the appeal of that damn lake up there. It's just a man-made lake. I think it's all a bunch of nonsense."

"True but like you said it's their money. Hey, I start class tomorrow at the junior college so you'll have to do more stuff for yourself. Can you do that for me? The nurse will still stop by and help you all she can."

"Yeah, I can do that. I wish I had a dog or something to break up the monotony of my day."

"I'll see what I can do. Does the paperman still toss the newspaper on the porch for you?"

"He has ever since I fell and broke my hip."

"That's good," Catawba replied as he got up.

He walked over to the refrigerator and opened the door. He looked at the fish sticks and milk and eggs and winced. He closed the door and turned to his grandfather.

"I don't see how you live off that diet."

"It's everything I need."

"Well, do you want me to cook you anything special or get you anything when I'm in town again?"

The old man offered no rejoinder as he turned around and took off through the house. Catawba followed him to the living room and watched him as he kicked off his shoes and laid down on the couch. He scratched his chin and looked up at his grandson.

"I'm going to take a nap," the old man said without emotion.

"I'll go then. Just remember I'm doing something nearly everyday now but I'll call you and stop by every chance I get."

He walked back through the house and went out the backdoor. He got in his car and headed home.

He went outside in the cool of the evening and walked around the yard looking at the greenery. The wisteria was in full bloom and the air smelled ambrosial. He stopped near the porch and watched the bumblebees going to and fro pollinating the purple flowers. The cat followed him a short distance off, jumping on grasshoppers, and sharpening his claws on the bark of a dogwood tree. He took off for a cedar tree near the end of the driveway but stopped when he heard someone yell. He heard it again and turned around and looked at the RV. He saw an arm waving to him from the door. He sighed and took off walking across the driveway.

When he got there he looked inside to see Don. He was shirtless and sitting on a plastic bucket while smoking a joint of immense size. To his right was a laminate coffee table and on the table was a plastic gallon bag containing something that looked like mulch.

"How's it going today Catawba?"

41

"I'm fine Don. How 'bout yourself?"

"I can't complain."

"I like what you've done with the place. The flags really improve the exterior of the RV."

"Thank you. Collecting flags is my hobby. Do you see that one," Don asked as he pointed up at the ceiling.

Catawba stepped back a few feet from the door and looked up at the top of the RV. He looked back at Don, shook his head and walked back to the door.

"Which one are you talking about?"

"The blue one with the red star on it."

"Of course I do," Catawba replied dryly.

"That's the flag for the Quebec Liberation Front. It took me years to find that one."

"It's nice. I guess."

"And what are your hobbies?"

"I like reading and writing and being outside in nature but people always seem to get in the way of that."

"Well shame on them for bothering you. Here, try some," Don said as he tried to pass the joint.

"No. No thank you. I'd rather not."

"Don't worry, it's medicinal."

Catawba rolled his eyes and grabbed the joint and took a big drag. He coughed and spit and handed it back with anger.

"What the hell was that? Cayenne pepper and dirt?"

"No sir, that's the best pot money can buy."

"I bet it is and where's Janice at today ?"

"She's swimming. She swims every day at the pool."

"And where's there a pool at around here?"

"Over that way," he said, motioning towards the road.

Catawba looked at the road and back at Don. He studied him for a moment and then took off for his house. He went inside and headed to the bathroom sink. He stood there brushing his teeth as the clock on the wall ticked away a soft cadence.

He was awakened the next morning by the kneading of the cat. He tried to push him off but he persisted until he got up and fed him. Then he made coffee and sat drinking it as he read a donated newspaper. In the paper there was an article about the future of the city's historic courthouse but nothing more. He finished his coffee, washed out his cup, and went to his desk. He tossed the textbook and a few other items in his rucksack and left.

When he got to the junior college he had to circle the campus a few times before he found the right building. He parked in front of a sober looking brick structure and got out. He went inside and found the right classroom but the door was locked. Too early, he thought as he looked down at his watch. He sat his rucksack down against the wall and retraced his steps.

He went outside and found an asphalt path next to the parking lot. He followed it down to a small pond where a trio of wood ducks paddled about. He looked around and tried to find a rock to skip but only found acorn shards. Then he took off walking around the pond. He stopped on the far side to inspect a couple of spavined kayaks on the bank. He nudged one of them with his toe of shoe and continued on and finished the loop around the water. He crossed back over the path and started whistling as he headed for the badminton courts a piece off. As he drew near the courts he saw a skeletal man in a boonie hat. He was standing beside the netting and fumbling with a clipboard. He looked up as Catawba walked onto the court.

"The walking class doesn't start for another hour," the man said.

"I'm just looking around and killing time. If that's alright."

"It's a free country."

"Do people really pay money and take time out of their lives to attend walking classes?"

"Uh," the man replied with a slight chuckle, "they have to. That or take another one of my classes. It's a mandatory requirement here at the school. My name is Dansberry Crowder and I teach all the outdoor classes here. You may have heard of me. I've been in the newspaper before."

"No," Catawba replied quickly as he shook his head, "I've never heard of you before. What did you do?"

"I won the world championship in kayaking eight years in a row."

"Really? You're a world champion kayaker?"

"That's right," he replied with a big grin.

"Well Crowder I just came from the pond and there was a vagrant
down there trying to wrestle one of those old things into the water."

"Are you shitting me?"

"No sir. I would never do such a thing. I told him to stop but he yelled something nasty so I walked up here."

Crowder dropped the clipboard and took off sprinting toward the pond. Catawba watched him disappear out of sight, then he smiled and walked on.

After a few minutes he came to a breezeway between two buildings. He stopped and stood there watching as students, yoked with backpacks, walked slowly by whispering to one another. Then he looked out over the campus to the pastureland that bordered the buildings. He took a few steps that way before it hit him that he had to get back. He turned around and took off walking with celerity as the day started to grow hot.

He grabbed his rucksack and walked into the classroom to see that the walls were covered with inspirational quotes on posters. He picked a seat close to the end and waited. Two other students walked in and sat down together. He reached down, got out the textbook, and sat it on top of the desk. He looked up to see a young woman enter the room. She had high cheekbones and her pecan colored hair was in a chignon. She walked over and sat down at the desk next to him. He glanced at her a time or two before turning her way.

"Hi, my name is Catawba and I like nature. What's your name?"

"I'm Nevena," she replied in a thick accent.

"That's a very beautiful accent you have. Where are you from?"

"I'm from that way," she said, pointing to the east.

"That's cool. I'm from here if you couldn't tell."

"Oh yes, I can tell. Can I ask you a question, Catawba?"

"Sure, by all means."

"Are you a shut in? Are you a recluse?"

"Of course not. I love society with all my heart. Why do you ask?"

"Because you're the most socially awkward person I have ever met."

"No, I mean I spend a lot of time alone in the woods. See, I'm a nature writer and park ranger trainee."

"If you say so."

"What do you do Nevena?"

"I'm a..."

Their eyes shot forward as a Methuselah aged instructor ambled through the door and up to the podium. He cleared his throat twice as he stood there fiddling with his papers. Then he looked at the clock on the wall behind him and back at the class.

"I think it's time we begin. My name is Professor Binetti and this class is entitled The English Language and You. We met every Wednesday for an hour during the six week summer semester. This is a personal enrichment class and not for credit. I see four students and my roll lists that very number. I want everybody to tell me their name, their favorite author, and why they are taking this class," he said as he glanced back and forth at the students.

He pointed at one of the students on the other side of the classroom. She cleared her throat and turned to face the others.

"My name is Theresa and I don't really read enough to have a favorite author. I'm just taking this class because I am retired and I need something to do this summer."

"That's okay Theresa, you're very straightforward and I like that," Binetti said as he turned to the next student.

"My name is Bethany and I am taking this class because I need to improve my writing skills. I'm in charge of writing the family newsletter."

"Do you have a favorite author?"

"No, not really. I do like reading the Dear Gabby column."

"That's fine. We are not all meant to read the classics. You'll find that I can more than help you with writing."

"And you young lady?"

"My name is Nevena and I like Charles Dickens. I need to become more proficient with writing in English for my business."

"That's a good choice young lady. Dickens was, in my mind, the apotheosis of the Victorian era."

"And you sir?"

"My name is Catawba and I like Henry David Thoreau. I guess I'm here to improve the elasticity of my poetic mind."

"I see," Binetti said, staring at him. "You like Thoreau?"

"Did I say something wrong sir?"

"No young master Catawba, it's just that Thoreau was an idler and hermit who lived alone in a cabin near a pond. He spent his days wandering around in the woods trying to avoid any meaningful social interaction."

"Well it sounds like he discovered the secret to true happiness."

"What did you say young man?" Binetti asked loudly.

"Um, what I meant to say sir, is that people are necessary for a functional, polite, and democratic society."

Binetti shook his head and sighed. He looked down at the lectern and fingered through his papers. He stopped after a moment and looked up.

"I want everyone to read the first chapter today in class and before we go we will talk about the first assignment which is due next week."

Catawba opened the textbook and sat there absentmindedly as he listened to Nevena breathing. He glanced her way a time or two but said nothing. After forty minutes he looked up to see that Binetti had left the room.

"Hey Nevena," he whispered.

"What Catawba?"

"Do they have ducks where you're from?"

"I don't know. I'm from the city," she said as she turned toward him, "but I know a skunk when I see one. Why do you ask?"

"I'm just curious. See, I'm a Renaissance man and good with a variety of subjects. If you come up to the lake where I work I can show you all the various plants and animals that this part of the country has to offer."

"If I can get off I might come," she replied meekly.

"What is it that you do again?"

"I..."

Their faces shot forward as the professor re-entered the door. He shuffled up to the lectern and looked at them one by one.

"Okay class. The first chapter was on the essay. Did everyone read it?"

Binetti looked around the room at the nods of approval. He uncapped his pen and looked down. He made a few marks and then looked up again.

"I want each of you to pick a social ill that you feel is destroying the world and write a three page essay on it."

Binetti went around the room asking for their essay subjects. Catawba didn't hear the topics of the other two but when the professor got to Nevena he heard her pick public health. Binetti wrote her down topic and looked up at him.

"Deforestation," he said loudly.

"Very well class. I will see you all next week."

He put his book and pencil in his rucksack and stood up. He walked out of the classroom quickly and headed for the door. He went outside and looked around for her but she was gone. Then he went over to his car and got in and headed home.

When he got there he tossed his rucksack on the porch and headed for the old shed. He undid the door clasp and opened the door. He pulled his bicycle out by the handlebars and headed for the road. He stopped at the end of the driveway, looked both ways, and hopped on. He pedaled out onto the road and started to pick up speed.

He waved to his neighbors, small children, and a one-eyed beagle as raced for the end of his road. He got there in no time and jumped off the bike to let a string of work trucks go by. After the last truck passed he remounted, turned left and headed out the dam road.

He rode over the first earthen dam, over the spillway bridge, and onto the power generation dam. He slowed down a few times to look out across the lake at the mountain faces coruscating in the sun. When he got to the end of the last dam

47

he pulled off onto a gravel service road. He walked his bike around the orange cones and pushed it into the woods. He camouflaged it with a few branches from a small oak tree and went back out to the gravel road. He walked down the gravel to the perimeter gate, read the no trespassing signs, and shook his head as he went around the thing.

The sun was high in the sky and the air was hot as he double timed it down a small hill with deep ruts and waterbars. A few frantic insects buzzed around his head and he swatted at them with his hands. He got to a big bend in the road and veered off of it into a small field of foxtail and then stopped to catch his breath at the base of a steep grade. He wiped the sweat from his forehead and started clambering up a big hill dotted with pine saplings. He crouched when he got to the top of the ridge and listened to the mechanized sounds from the other side.

When the noise lulled a bit he peeked over and grunted at what he saw. Acres of forest in every direction lay desolated by the power company. He tried to count the logging trucks and the harvesters and the delimbers but their serpentine movements stymied him. After an hour he retreated back down the hill. He went back up the gravel road to his bicycle, pitched the limbs off his bike, and pushed it back to the road. Then he got on and started pedaling back to his house.

A few minutes later he zipped into his yard. He leaned the bike against the house and went inside to type his paper.

8

He got up Friday morning at dawn. He tossed some vittles and water in his rucksack and strapped his best hikers to his feet. He shouldered his rucksack and headed for the door. He went outside and grabbed the bicycle and pushed it to the road. He hopped on and started pedaling up the road toward the park entrance.

When he got to the park office he found the place deserted. He climbed off the bicycle and leaned it up against the side of the building. He adjusted his pack and walked over to the edge of the sidewalk and looked out across the lake. The sunbeams were just beginning to illuminate the clear waters near the beach and the Carolina chickadees serenaded loudly at the approaching day. He smiled but that smile quickly vanished when heard a sound coming from behind him. He turned around to see an old hooptie truck with a park service logo barreling toward the office.

The truck stopped about ten feet away from the sidewalk and a gangly man with grey hair stepped out. He put on a pair of aviator sunglasses and walked to the front of the truck and leaned across the hood. He lit a cigarette, exhaled a big plume of smoke, and smiled.

"Say, you must be Catawba, I'm Vance. Just toss your things in the back of the truck and we'll be ready to roll."

"Thank you, Yeah Ranger Lansing said that you were…"

"Yes sir," Vance said, cutting him off, "I am your compatriot in all things pertaining to the park service. I was a trail worker in Denali, a fire lookout in the Cascades, heck, I even led donkey tours in the Grand Canyon. Did you ever hear about the big fire they had in Yellowstone back in eighty-eight?"

"I wasn't even aware of Yellowstone back then," he replied.

"I drove a pump truck for thirty-four straight hours during the peak of the battle. Yes sir, the park service named a wilderness latrine after me for my meritorious service."

Catawba nodded his head and put his rucksack in the toolbox. Then he stood there for a minute looking at Vance before getting in the truck. Vance took one long last drag from his cancer stick and walked over and flicked it into the mulch. He walked back and climbed in the truck with Catawba.

"Say Vance. Don't you think you need to be more careful with cigarettes around here?"

"Nonsense," he replied as he buckled up.

He looked over at Catawba in his mirrored sunglasses, smiled, and put the truck in gear. They drove away and headed down one of the paved arteries of the park.

"Where are we going?" Catawba asked after a mile.

"We have a route. We clean the campground first. Then we clean the picnic area and we finish out the day doing crowd control and interacting with the visitors. Just look out for any unattended fires in the vicinity," he said as he dug around for his cigarettes. "Hey, let me tell you a story about the time I worked for the park service up in Maine."

Catawba sat there listening and enjoying the ride as Vance talked away.

They pulled up in front of a cedar boarded bathhouse and got out together. Vance went over and unlocked the janitor's closet as Catawba stood there watching him. He went inside and pushed out the cleaning cart.

"Here you go amigo. Go knock out the men's side and I'll stand here at the door and make sure no one tries to come in."

"Okay Vance."

He pushed the cart to the door, opened it and pulled it in. He found a disgusting scene of dirt, trash, and soap scum. He grabbed the broom and started cleaning. He swept everything to the center of the room, pushed it into a big metal dustpan, and dumped it. After that he got out a scouring pad and abrasive cleaning powder and scrubbed down the fixtures until they shined like new dimes. Then he replenished the paper products and checked the shower valves for functionality. He finished up by pulling the trash bag and sitting it outside the door. He loaded up all the cleaning paraphernalia and pushed the cart back out the door. He found Vance standing next to a tree and fiddling with the walkie-talkie. He looked up at Catawba and smiled.

"This radio is on the fritz and we need it in case of an emergency situation. I'll work on it while you knock out the women's side."

Catawba gave him a caustic look and took the cart over to the other side. He opened the door and went in. The filthy scene was repeated for him again, but this time, it stunk to high heaven. He cleaned with celerity and then went back out. He pushed the cart into the closet and shut the door. He wiped the sweat from his forehead and looked around. Vance was nowhere to be found so he went over and sat down on a large granite rock at the edge of the parking lot.

After a while he heard footsteps in the brush and turned around to see Vance coming out of a laurel thicket. He stood up as Vance made a beeline for the truck.

"Is everything alright?"

"Yeah. I went to spy on the campers."

They got in the truck and headed into the campground. The tent sites were spaced fifty yards apart on the bosky peninsula and brimming with people of every age, race, and ethnicity. Vance drove out to the end of the long maintenance road and turned the truck around. He pulled up to the first set of trash cans and flipped on the hazard lights.

"I'll sit right here in the truck and make sure there are no issues with safety. You just get out there and check those bags. Change 'em if they need it. I've got your back little buddy."

"Uh, okay I guess," Catawba replied hesitantly.

He got out and checked the trash cans. The bags were brim full and heavy. He tied them off and slung them in the back of the truck. He put in new bags and sat the lids back on. When he tried to get back in the truck Vance waved him off and motioned at him to walk on to the next set. He sighed and resigned himself to the task ahead. He walked the entirety of the road, changing countless bags along the way. After the last bag he climbed back into the cab of the truck. The AC was roaring away and Vance was drumming his fingers on the steering wheel. Catawba stared at him and gritted his teeth. Vance smiled, turned the radio up, and took off.

They went to the park dumpsters and unloaded the bags. Vance told him they would take a small break before going on to the group picnic area. Catawba agreed and they stood there for a while, him sipping water and Vance telling some cock-and-bull story that he himself probably didn't even believe. Then they loaded up again and headed on.

The sun was high in the sky and the heat was rising up from the asphalt as they sailed down the main park road toward the group picnic area. They crossed the big timber bridge that spanned Irish Creek and climbed the hill to the top of the ridge. They slowed near the parking lot of the mountain bike trails to let several pedestrians pass. Then they continued on until they came to the service road of the massive picnic area. Catawba hopped out and opened the gate.

They drove to the end of the picnic area and parked. The sites were filled to capacity and the air smelled of grilled meat and maize. Vance got a small bucket and trash picker out of the toolbox and handed it to Catawba. He took it and started picking up the bottle caps, cigarette butts, and other waste from the ground. After a few minutes he turned around to see Vance lollygagging with the kids of a large Hispanic family. He chuckled, shook his head, and continued on.

They finished cleaning the picnic area in two hours and hauled the trash off to the dumpsters.

"Time for lunch," Vance said as he was driving back to the park office.

"Okay."

"You can go eat by the lake or sit in the breezeway at the office."

"That sounds good."

"Meet me at the truck in an hour."

Vance parked the truck in front of the office and got out and went inside. Catawba grabbed his rucksack and h urried off to the covered picnic shed. He sat down at a defaced picnic table and dug out a fruit cup, a piece of string cheese, and a lukewarm bottle of water. He opened the fruit cup and down it in a single gulp. He tore open the cheese and parceled it out in front of him. Then he sat there having little nuggets of cheese and sips of water as he watched the hikers stop at the information board close by.

When he finished eating he stood up and looked out at the lake cove. A few fishing boats drifted to and fro, casting and reeling their lines in cadences all their own. He wiped the sweat from his brow and looked down at his watch. He grabbed his rucksack and headed back to the truck. He put his pack away and looked over at the office. He didn't see any movement so he took off down the path toward the beach. He stopped in the sand and looked around at all the children playing and screaming. He heard the flicking of a lighter and turned around to see Vance watching him.

"What are you doing?"

"I was just watching the beach. I didn't see you."

"You're not ready for beach patrol yet. Let's go."

"Okay."

They went back to the truck and got in. Vance drove him to the campground and told him to get out. Catawba hopped out and got his pack out of the toolbox.

"What do you want me to do?"

"I want you to spend the afternoon in the campground assisting the visitors. I'll come get you when it's time to get off. Here, take this radio."

"Okay, I can do that," he replied as he grabbed the radio.

Catawba stood there watching as Vance drove off like a flash of lightning. Then he put the radio in his rucksack and strapped it to his back. He took off walking into the campground as the sweat started to seep through his park shirt.

At the first campsite he found a couple trying their best to untangle the webbing that went to a hammock. He stopped and watched them for a while until they turned around and looked at him.

"Do you guys need me? I'm from the park service and I'm here to help."

"No," the man said irately, "we're just practicing our knot knowledge."

"That's fine," he replied happily, "If you need me I'll be walking around here helping people with their camping quandaries."

He walked on until he came to a collapsed retaining wall. He sat his pack down on the ground and dug out a half full bottle of water. He stood there sipping it and feeling unneeded until he felt a tug on the back of his shirt. He turned around to see a tall woman in a bathing suit looking at him.

"Yes mam, how can I help you?"

"There is poison ivy at my campsite. Can you remove it?"

"Maybe you shouldn't be in a park if that kind of thing worries you."

"What the hell? Who are you?"

"My name is Catawba Fox and I am a seasonal park ranger. I will go check it out but I cannot cut it down. That would probably violate some government regulation."

"Fine," she said.

53

He grabbed his pack up off the ground and they took off walking together to the nearest campsite. She had a red tent spread out in the leaves and nothing else. She walked over to a tree behind the tent and pointed at a green vine climbing up the trunk. Catawba walked over and looked up at it. He rubbed his forehead and sighed.

"That's wisteria and it is perfectly harmless."

"I know it is poison ivy and I know you're lying to me. I'm going to call your supervisor when I get the chance."

"Well you do what you think is best. I'm going to go help people who actually need it," he replied as he walked away.

He walked on and cut up a steep hill and came upon a big pile of pine firewood. The wood was rotting and fence lizards darted back and forth across the disintegrating bark. He wiped the sweat from his forehead and took off walking through a stand of yellow pines toward the lake. When he got to the shore he sat down on a stump and looked out across the water.

A pontoon boat floated listlessly in the channel as the occupants took photos of the rocky escarpments to the west. Then he looked toward the cement dam and saw a man paddling a homemade coracle. He watched him for a while before looking toward the far shore where a group of canoeists paddled quickly along as if part of some combat flotilla.

He got up when the excitement petered out, dusted off his backside, and headed back to the campground. He found the place frantic with people carrying in their camping gear. He stood in the busiest part of the footpath but no one spoke to him and no one noticed him. After a long time he looked down at his watch and headed back to the parking lot.

He was sitting on a rock whistling a sea shanty when Vance pulled up in the park truck and motioned at him to get in. He got up and put his rucksack in the back of the truck. He opened the truck door and felt a big burst of cool air. He climbed inside and closed the door.

Vance drove back to the park office quickly and talked even quicker. Catawba tried to listen and he even tried to care but he grew tired of the ceaseless nattering and just started nodding his head.

He got out when the truck stopped, grabbed his things, and walked over to his bike. He put the rucksack on the seat and kicked up the kickstand. Then he shouldered his pack and climbed on and started pedaling. A hazy heat rose up from the asphalt and the traffic whizzed by him without hesitation during the three mile ride home.

He zipped into the driveway and got off. He carried the bike up on the porch and went inside. He dropped his rucksack on the floor as he headed for the kitchen. He went to the kitchen sink and poured himself a big glass of cold water and stood there drinking it as the cat swiped his legs. Then he went to his bed and collapsed in a wave of exhausted torpidity.

9

The next day, after they got done cleaning the park, Vance drove them to the parking lot of the mountain bike trails. They got out and walked around picking up the little pieces of litter on the ground. Vance smoked and talked away as he trudged along while Catawba tried to follow his lectures about all things wild and free. When they got done they tossed the litter in a trashcan and went back to the truck. Vance dug a trash bag out of the toolbox and handed it to Catawba.

"Get your backpack out. After you eat your lunch I want you to go check for trash on the mountain bike trails," Vance said forcefully.

"My god man there's fifteen miles of trail."

"Do your best. I have faith in you."

Catawba didn't say anything as he got his rucksack out and tied the trash bag to it. Vance smiled at him, got in the truck, and took off. Catawba stood there watching as the vehicle disappeared down the dusty park road. Then he kicked a rock with the toe of his shoe and started walking down the shaded trail.

He walked for a while until he came upon a treey bottomland that butted up against the lake. The trunks were painted ocher from the silt of a recent flood and the ground was littered with leaves and shore scree. He cut toward the lake but stopped when he came upon a small pile of rubble. He inspected the rocks and decided it was a stone foundation from some ancient structure.

He sat down on a log, looked at his watch, and took out his canteen. He uncapped it and took a long pull of water as he listened to the sounds of the bikes and the birds.

When he finished off the canteen he put it back in his pack and stood up. He looked around and took off for a small wooded peninsula that was directly ahead of him. He started to step across a small rill when something caught his eyes. He stopped and squatted down against the moist dirt as he studied the peculiar shape going through the brush. He listened and heard a faint humming emanating from the object. Then he stood up, stepped over the rill, and took off after the anomaly.

He climbed up a small embankment and found himself in the midst of a laurel thicket looking at the backside of a park ranger in a safari hat. He was tall and peering through a set of black binoculars at the lake. He took a few stealthy steps but the crunching of the dried leaves hooked the ranger's attention. He turned around and looked at Catawba.

"Hey there buddy," the ranger said with a nasally voice.

"I didn't mean to scare you sir," Catawba replied.

"You're not bothering me. I'm looking out at the osprey platform. Here look."

Catawba grabbed the binoculars and looked out to a small barren island next to the lake channel where a metal pole and platform rose some twelve feet into the air. He stood there for a moment looking out at the platform but didn't see the osprey so he handed the glasses back.

"I don't see them."

"That's because they're not there. My name is John Quincey," he said as he proffered a hand.

"Nice to meet you," he replied as they shook. "I'm Catawba and I'm working here this summer."

"That's nice. You see Catawba, the osprey is notorious for returning to the same nesting platform year after year. The fact that they're not here this year is a little bit troubling. I would tell the park ornithologist but alas I am the park ornithologist. Do you like birds?"

"I like owls and ducks sir but probably not on your level."

"That's nice. You see Catawba, I am a connoisseur and lover of all things feathery. From hunting grouse and duck all across North America to going on vacation in Papua New Guinea where I trekked through the rainforest to watch the mating behavior of the birds-of-paradise."

"That doesn't make any sense."

"What? What doesn't make any sense?" Quincey asked sharply.

"What I meant to say sir is that a man of your expertise should be on the cover of every biological publication this great country has to offer."

"Yes, that sounds better. And what are you doing here in the woods? Shouldn't you be in the picnic area helping the visitors?"

"Vance told me to walk the mountain bike trails and look for trash."

"Catawba, how much waste can a mountain bike make?"

"I'm only doing what I'm told to do sir."

"That's nice. Now you go back out to the parking lot and wait for Vance. I've got this."

He nodded and headed back out. He went down the embankment and hopped over the rill. He walked through the bottomland and then followed the trail up and out to the parking lot. When he got there he looked down at his watch and shook his head. He wiped the sweat out of his eyes and took off jogging down the road toward the park office.

Vance was climbing in the truck when he got back to the parking lot. He yelled out and Vance stopped.

"I got sent back here by Quincey," he said when he got close to the truck.

"Where did you run into him at ?"

"He was out on the peninsula next to the bike trails. He was looking across the lake at an osprey platform but they weren't there. He is the strangest person I've ever met. Vance, can I ask you a question I've had for the last hour?"

"Sure," he replied as he fumbled with his cigarettes.

"If you really liked birds, why would you kill them?"

"Yeah," he replied halfheartedly, "I know what you mean about that."

A door slammed on the office and they turned around to see Ranger Lansing standing atop the back steps looking at them. He stuck his finger out and pointed at Catawba. He sighed and walked over to him.

"Yes sir?"

"How do you like working here? This is your second day so you should know by now."

"It is a very interesting occupation. A new challenge awaits me daily. I think I am a valuable asset to the general public and a friend to all visitors great and small."

"Cut the shit," he said in a whisper. "Is Vance screwing off or not?"

"No sir, Vance is shepherding me towards the promised land."

"That's good. I like to hear good things about the staff. Now make sure you fill out your timesheet and let me know if any problems arise."

He nodded his head and went back over to Vance. He was smoking away and watching a trio of nubiles saunter down the path toward the beach. He stood there for a moment and then cleared his throat. Vance snapped around and looked at him.

"I'm going home now," he said.

Vance didn't say anything so he went over to the bike rack. He got his bike out and climbed on and started pedaling home.

10

The next morning he arrived at the park office to find a shiny park service SUV in the staff parking lot. He dismounted and leaned his bike up against the wall. He looked around but didn't see Vance or the truck. He took off walking for the beach but a booming voice behind him stopped him in his tracks

"Catawba Fox," roared a stranger's voice.

"What," he yelled back.

58

He turned around to see a short man in a ranger hat goose stepping his way. He stood there watching the man's approach and trying to keep from laughing at his footwork.

"I am Superintendent Mooseberg," the man snapped when he got close to him, "and you follow me right up here to my office immediately. We have to go over an incident that was reported to us by a park visitor."

Catawba didn't say anything. He just took off for the park office with Mooseburg nipping at his heels like a Jack Russell Terrier. He went up the back steps, opened the door, and disappeared inside. Ranger Lansing was sitting at the window reading a sportsmans periodical and looking terrified. Catawba stood there looking around at the office interior as Mooseburg walked into his private office and sat down.

"Mr. Fox, please come in here and shut the door."

He went into the office and shut the big thick wooden door. He sat down in an office chair and looked around as Mooseburg began banging away on the keyboard. There were pennants from various sports teams and photos of Mooseburg on vacation in exotic locations plastered all over the walls.

"Take your backpack off Mr. Fox. You're staying put today," Mooseburg said.

"Okay sir."

He took his rucksack off and sat it on the floor. He got his canteen out and took a few sips while the boss typed away on the keyboard. At last Mooseburg turned and gave him a fiery look.

"Okay. We need to have an employee counseling session. You have violated park service regulations. We got a report that on your first day you were disrespectful to a park visitor who had a question about the native plants in the area. Do you remember this?"

"I remember some idiot in the campground asking me about poison ivy and I told them…"

"Don't call them idiots Mr. Fox, they're taxpayers. Go on."

"Superintendent Mooseburg the camper mistook wisteria for poison ivy," he replied humbly.

"Now that may be so, but we have rules here, the park service has rules. Only a certified Botanist is qualified to make that determination and if one is not available we are to consult the regional guidebook that is issued by the government."

"Uh, I think I know what grows in the woods around here."

"No you dont."

"Uh okay, and how would I go about getting myself a regional handbook?"

"You would have to go to the yearly seminar in the fall but since you are seasonal staff you wouldn't qualify."

"Well what do you want me to do then?"

"Just profess your stupidity to people who ask questions. That's what we do and it usually makes them go away."

"Is that all?"

"Nope," Mooseburg said bluntly. "Ranger Quincey said you were wandering around in the woods when you should have been helping visitors. He said you interfered with his raptor research project."

"Am I in trouble sir?"

"I am giving you a written reprimand and I'm going to make you spend the morning watching a video on the proper conduct of seasonal employees."

Mooseburg sat a piece of paper down in front of him and gave him a pen. He read the first few lines and then signed it. Mooseburg hopped up and Catawba followed him as he went out the door and down the back steps. They went inside the basement where a TV was sitting on a rolling metal stand. Catawba grabbed a folding chair, put it down in front of the TV, and took a seat.

He sat there in silence watching as his boss rifled through the old VHS tapes on the stand. After a few moments Mooseburg found the one he wanted and pushed it into the slot. The black screen turned blue and the tape started to play. Mooseburg watched for a split second before darting back outside. The VHS tape froze and skipped and then ejected itself out of the slot. It landed on the laminate floor in front of him with a little whiff of smoke. He looked around and listened but heard nothing. He got up slowly, tip-toed to the TV stand, and started looking through the tapes. He didn't see anything he liked until he came across a documentary on the whooping crane. He pushed the tape into the slot and sat back down.

A narrator came on the screen and began a heartfelt presentation on how the whooping crane was being pushed to the edge of extinction because of overhunting and loss of habitat. After that the narrator went on to talk about how only a handful remained in the wild and how efforts to recover the species had thus far been limited. The video ended with a picture of the majestic cranes flying over the marshlands of Texas. "That's awful," he whispered.

He got up when the credits started to roll and walked to the VCR. He took the tape out and went out the basement door. He walked up the back steps and headed inside. He went into the superintendent's office as Mooseberg sat typing away at the keyboard. Catawba picked up his rucksack and looked over at him.

"Eat your lunch then spend the rest of the day in the picnic area assisting visitors. That will be all Mr. Fox," Mooseburg said without looking at him.

"Will do."

He walked out of the office, through the parking lot, and down to the boat dock. He took off his shoes and socks and sat down with his feet in the cool water.

I'm not going to make it here, he thought. He sat there thinking about all the fleeting moments of human existence squandered with bureaucratic minutiae and foolish officialdom but then he snapped out when he felt something nibbling at his big toe. He looked down at the water and noticed minnows darting back and forth around his foot. He laughed and turned around and dug his pencil and pad out of his rucksack. He wetted the tip end of the pencil and started making a plan.

When he got done writing he looked at his watch. He put his things away, strapped his shoes back on his feet, and stood up. He could hear the throngs of people gathered for their Sunday afternoon picnics. He shouldered his rucksack and marched off to meet the challenge.

He entered the picnic area and stopped at the first site. A sooty-faced homunculus stood there with a stick slowly stirring the exhausted ashes of the grill. Catawba asked him if he needed help but the answer he got was in a tongue he couldn't comprehend. He nodded his head and walked on.

He went to the center of the picnic area and took in the scene. Groups of men from all races and climes were gathered around their grills while the family matriarchs nibbled on raw vegetables and stood watch over the babies. Teenage boys and girls traded libidinous looks as they awaited their chance to disappear into the humid woods.

He found a flat rock next to a poplar tree and sat down. He wiped the sweat from his face and started sipping water from his canteen.

Only a handful of times during the afternoon did anyone ask him a question or acknowledge his existence. During the last hour an old man brought him a full cup of cold horchata. He thanked him and killed the liquid in one long gulp. The old man offered no reply as he took the cup back and shuffled away.

He stood up at the exact minute his day was done. He scanned the families and started to walk back. As he drew close to the office he noticed a gargantuan sized man with a potbelly and ponytail coming out of the office. He picked up speed when he saw the park service insignia on the man's shirt.

"Hello there," he said loudly when he got within a few steps of him, "my name is Catawba Fox and I'm a new seasonal employee here."

"Nice to meet you. My name's Lenny and I'm in charge of the entire maintenance department around here."

"Nice to meet you too. I hate to bother you but I am supposed to meet Ranger Quincey at his personal vehicle after work. Do you know what he drives?"

"Of course I do, he drives the canary yellow wagon. He always parks that thing at the maintenance shop up on the ridge."

"Thank you Lenny."

"No problem. Say, what are you and Quincey doing after work?"

"I'm going to go help him with a nesting project. I am so glad someone like that would take me under their wing. If you get my drift."

"Yep," Lenny replied as he took off for his park truck.

Catawba watched him walk to his truck, get inside and leave. Then he walked over to the office door and disappeared inside. He found the seasonal timesheets on a clipboard and filled his out. He went back outside, climbed on his bike, and headed home.

He walked through the backdoor of his house and dropped his rucksack. He went to the kitchen and got out a lidded jar and sat it down on the formica countertop. He reached into the cupboard and brought a canister of dried oats and two cans of Alaskan salmon. He filled the jar half full of oats and drained the salmon juice on top. He closed the lid on the jar and carried it to the sunny sided windowsill. He sat it down and heard a sound coming from behind him. He turned around to see the cat switching his tail.

"Looks like everyone is having fish for a while."

11

When the alarm clock went off he shot out of bed, put on his clothes and donned his good walking shoes. He went to the kitchen and had a big glass of water. He sat the cup down and grabbed the jar of oats from the windowsill. They were bloated and caramel colored and he smiled as he stood there shaking them up. He put them into the crook of his arm and went outside and disappeared into the false dawn of the day.

He came back inside the house just as the clock on the wall struck eight. He got out some potatoes and cubed them and put them on a metal baking sheet. He lathered them down with olive oil and sprinkled them with salt and pepper and fresh thyme. He slid them in the oven, turned the heat dial and looked at his watch. Then he walked to his desk and sat down with a book.

After an hour passed he got up and went to the kitchen. He took the pan out of the oven and sat it on the countertop. He grabbed the dish towel and fanned the potatoes until he thought they were manageable. Then he put them in a covered dish and carried them outside and climbed into the car.

He pulled up behind his grandfather's house, grabbed the bowl, and went inside. He found the old man sitting barefoot at the kitchen table reading the newspaper. He waved at him with the bowl as he walked into the room. He put it in the refrigerator and sat down at the head of the table and looked over at his grandfather. After a few minutes the old man sat the paper aside, turned toward his grandson, and let out a long sigh.

"Catawba did you know they were going to destroy that huge hayfield and all the farmland down there next to the junior college?"

"No Pop, I didn't. Who told you that?"

"It's in the newspaper today. They say the state is going to build a school of robotics."

"I think someone is pulling your leg. I was down there last week and it looked fine to me."

"Here look at the paper," the old man said as he reached for the paper.

"No," he said as he waved it off, "I never have a good day after I read that trash. I get sick of their gentrification nonsense."

"What's gen... genifergation?"

"Gentrification. It's where they destroy a community piece by piece and person by person until there is nothing left."

"I never knew that."

"Well don't worry about it. That word is much too honest for that organization to print."

"Oh."

"Anyway, I brought you some potatoes I baked this morning. Olive oil and thyme, just like you like them. Did you know the power company is clearing even more land below the dams?"

"I figured as much. I can see the main highway from the porch and sometimes it is nothing but logging trucks."

"Pop, I cycled over there the other day and walked down the gravel road. They're cutting down all the trees that are hidden from the road."

"Catawba, just let it go. There is nothing either one of us can do about it. How's the job at the park service going?"

He chuckled as he got up and got a glass of water. He downed it in a few swallows and wiped his mouth with the back of his hand. He turned around and looked at his grandfather.

"Did you know a group of skunks is called a surfeit?"

"No I didn't. I'm a happy person if those things leave me alone. Why do you ask?"

"I'm wanting to start a surfeit of skunks to skedaddle a skunk back to skunkville ."

"Is that some nursery rhythm?"

"No. No it's not. It's just a little diddy I wrote while I was out on my jaunt this morning."

"Well it will certainly entertain children if you ever have them."

"I guess so. Now, I'll come by and mow your grass Wednesday after class."

The old man didn't say anything as he pushed himself up from the table and put his hands on the walker and took off for the living room. Catawba followed behind him watching his unsteady movements. He sat down in a straight backed chair and grabbed the remote.

"Pop, did you hear me?"

"Yeah. You're going to go mow the grass."

"No. I'm going to do it after class Wednesday."

"How's that?"

"How's what? I'll use the mower," he replied.

"No. How's the class going? Are you getting your money's worth out of that place?"

"I'm getting there. I'll be rich and respectable by the end of the semester."

"That's nice," he replied as he turned on the TV.

Catawba looked at him for a moment before taking off back through the house. He went out the backdoor and into the rising heat of the morning. He walked over to his car and got in. He rolled down the windows, backed up, and set sail for town.

He drove down to the city on the backroads, looking out at the fertile gardens and taking in the luscious green fields. Cows stood by their fences awaiting their daily ration of hay and blathering bovine to any ears that would listen.

When he reached the city limits he cut down the bypass and headed for the health foods store. He parked in front of the building, got out and went inside, and started looking at the placards. He made an educated guess and went down an end aisle. He walked slowly, looking at the tinctures and tonics. He stopped halfway down and picked up a brown glass bottle and studied the label. "That'll do," he whispered.

"Sir, may I help you?" asked a voice from behind him.

He turned around to see a young associate staring at him. He looked at her name tag and scratched the back of his neck.

"Um, I'm getting some fish oil for work. I think I found what I'm looking for."

"Oh so you need more energy for work?"

"No. My energy is fine. I'm treating a varmint problem. The woods are full of them."

"Sir, we have a large selection of essential oils that will repel most any nuisance you may encounter."

"Can I ask you a question miss ?"

"That's what I'm here for," she replied meekly.

"Essential oils. Do they work?"

"I wouldn't know to tell you the truth. They make me sneeze but we do sell a lot of them to the people who move here."

"That's what I thought. I think I'm just going to have to stick with this."

He walked to the front to pay as she dashed past him to the register. She worked the buttons and scanned the oil. She told him the price and he handed over the money. She gave him his change and he nodded as he picked up the bag. He went outside and took off walking towards the new fitness center.

When he got there he saw that the outside looked the same. He peeped through the glassdoor but nothing moved inside the darkened interior. He turned around and hurried on. He headed up the street to the hill that overlooked the center of the town. He stopped at the top and looked over at the historic courthouse lawn. There was flagging tied around the trees but he couldn't make out its meaning. He let it go and walked back to his vehicle and left for home.

That evening, after he had got through eating, he decided to turn on the TV. He flipped through the basic cable channels until he came across the public access station. The station was showing profiles of local citizens who had made something of themselves in the world. He sat there with complete indifference until the final segment of the broadcast. "I'll be damned," he said loudly as he sat up straight in the chair.

His best friend from grade school appeared on the screen. He was standing in the East Wing of the White House with a medal around his neck and smiling as the president addressed a large audience.

"And this young man right here," the president said with great energy, "is a model American. He grew up in a tough town in the middle of nowhere. He pulled himself out the gutter by sheer determination and went on to start a tech firm that created a rideshare app that is revolutionizing transportation in the twenty-first century. But ladies and gentleman all that was before he reached the age of thirty. When he hit thirty he purchased a zero-emissions yacht and decided to find himself out on the open ocean. He set a course to circle the world but he was met by a typhoon in the South China Sea. His yacht capsized and as he bobbed up and down in the water a massive tiger shark took a meaty chunk out of his ribcage. Now, most people would have thrown up their hands and died, but this young man, being a model American, took off swimming toward an island that was miles away. When he reached the shore he found that the place was crawling with fascists who were mere minutes away from launching a full scale invasion of the Western Hemisphere. Well folks, this young man killed them all with his bare hands as he hemorrhaged blood from the bite wound. Then he used their sick pamphlets to build a fire so he could send smoke signals to the U.S. Nav..."

He cut the TV off and staggered to his bedroom. He laid down on the bed and stared up at the ceiling and didn't move.

12

Wednesday morning he parked his car on the college campus and got out. The heat haze was already rising from the asphalt as he walked up to the building and opened the door. He went to the classroom and found the other students already seated. He sat down next to Nevena and put his textbook on top of the desk.

"Hi Catawba."

"Hi Nevena, did you have a good week?"

"Yes I did. I have a great many things to be excited about."

"That's good I guess. Don't let this heat get you down."

"It would never do such a thing. Did you not see what I am wearing?"

He turned to his left and looked at her. She was wearing a tank top and running shorts. He looked at her face and then turned slowly back to the front.

"I'm sorry Nevena, I didn't even pay attention to you when I sat down. I'm having a rough go of it this week."

"What happened?"

"I don't think I'm cut out to be a park ranger or writer. I'm probably not cut out to be a human being either. I would say I am a failure in that but failure probably has some requirements that even I couldn't meet."

She snickered and patted him on the back of the head.

"You'll be alright. I'll come see you at the lake sometime."

Their eyes shot forward as Binetti hobbled into the room and up to the lectern. He was wearing a sweater vest and carrying a tacky beige coffee cup. Catawba let out a long sigh and Nevena grinned as the other two students began peppering him with hokey compliments. He smiled as he listened to them and looked at the papers on the lectern. After a few moments he looked up.

"Okay class, how are we all today?"

"I'm great Mr. Binetti," answered Beth.

"That's marvelous," he replied.

"And everyone else?" Binetti asked as he looked at Nevena and Catawba.

"Catawba is not good," Nevena blurted out. "He says he is a loser in life."

"Catawba, is that true? Are you a loser?"

"No sir, I'm not a loser. Loser implies that somewhere there is a winner and that means that life is some kind of straightforward competition but it's not. Life is a war of attrition with circus clowns."

Binetti and Nevena burst out laughing as the other students sat there looking confused. Catawba half chuckled as he slid his essay out of his textbook.

"Okay class, today we are going to talk about how to edit your work," Binetti said before going up to the whiteboard.

During the next forty minutes he filled the whiteboard with the most banal items imaginable and asked questions along the way. Catawba watched Nevena as she took notes in Cyrillic and underlined things she deemed important. He tried to get her to talk but she would only purse her lips and shoot him malevolent glances.

Binetti capped the marker as time wound down and came back to the lectern. He looked around at the class and waited but was met with only silence.

"Okay, since we are all mature adults, I want you guys to swap papers and edit them for each other. Then next week you'll give them back to the owner and read the notes and changes suggested. Oh and I want you to read the next chapter on current events. That will be all."

Catawba tried to hand his paper to Nevena but she darted off to Teresa. He got up slowly and forced a smile as he walked over and traded with Beth. He walked back, gathered his things up, and went outside. He walked the sidewalk over to the end of the campus buildings and stopped. The old man was right, he thought.

He looked out at the sprawling farm fields and saw a bulldozer making passes and laying waste to everything green that lived. He winced and walked back to his car. He started the engine and left and headed up the road for his grandfather's house.

Two hours later he was standing in the door of the toolshed wiping grass clippings off the front of his hiking shorts. He closed the door and walked to the center of the yard. He looked at the ornamental windmill and noticed it was drooping to the side. He took his hands and tried to adjust the frame but it fell off and hit the ground. The windmill broke into pieces upon impact and a rotted blade rolled over onto the top of his shoe. He bent over, collected the pieces, and carried them to the porch. His grandfather came out of the house and looked at the decrepit contraption.

"Catawba Fox," the old man snapped, "did you hit my windmill with the mower?"

"No Pop I didn't. It was leaning over to the side and it fell off when I tried to fix it. I think we can glue it back together but if we can't we'll get another one."

"You'll not get another one of those. Obert made that for me fifty years ago and he's dead now."

"Sit down and let me look at it."

Catawba dropped to his knees with the parts and spread them out in front of him. He turned them over and inspected each one of them. The tailpiece was warped and most of the wooden blades were rotted beyond repair. He sighed and looked up at his grandfather.

"Hey Pop, this thing is gone," he said as he got up slowly. "I'm sorry but there is nothing I can do."

The old man didn't respond to what was said. He opened the screen door and disappeared inside the house. Catawba dropped to his knees again and picked up the pieces and took them to the porch swing. He turned around to see the old man coming out the door with a box in his hand. He waved at his grandson to move and he stepped aside and watched as the old man raked the pieces into the box. Then

70

he carried it back into the house with a determined gait. Catawba took off after him and followed him to the kitchen.

His grandfather dumped the broken windmill on the kitchen table and started looking at the various components. He rubbed his head and then went over to the cup cabinet and got out a small crusted bottle of glue and sat down. Catawba went to speak but stopped. He just stood there watching as the old man tried to fix the unfixable.

"That windmill really means a lot to you?"

"Catawba," the old man said without looking up, "the man who made this for me was an old man when I was a young man."

"Oh."

He tinkered with it until he lost interest, then he let out a long sigh and started looking out the window.

"Do you want me to carry it back out on the porch for you?"

"No. Just leave it alone."

"Okay I'm so sorry."

Catawba walked over and checked the food in the refrigerator. He opened up the cabinets and looked inside and checked the pill trays. Then he walked back to the table and put his hand on his grandfather's shoulder.

"You were right. The state is going to build something big down there in the hayfield next to the junior college. They've already started clearing the land. It looks like the thing is going to be pretty huge."

"That's good for them. I hope they can build something that makes windmills. I don't understand anything anymore."

"I'm so sorry Pop. Is there anything that I can do for you? You're all set on pills and food for the time being."

"Don't you remember what I wanted you to get me?"

"And what is that?"

"I ask you to get me a dog for company."

"Pop you can't walk around outside with a big dog on a leash but I'll see if I can get you a small dog."

"Okay, that's fine I guess."

"The nurse will be by soon so call me if you need me. I have to get home."

71

He left the tableside and went out the backdoor and got in his car and drove away. He found that the road back to his house was choked with trucks pulling boats to the lake.

He turned into the driveway and got out to get the mail but before he could shut his car door he heard a faint whimpering coming from the RV. He sighed and looked that way to see a pair of pasty white feet jutting out from inside. He shut his car door and started walking that way.

When he drew near he saw Don lying on the scuffed laminate flooring in nothing but his underwear. He was sweating profusely despite the fact that the little AC unit roared with all its might.

"What's wrong here neighbor?" he asked without any real concern.

"Catawba," Don said without moving, "I know you smoked all my pot."

"No Don, I didn't smoke your dope. Are you alright though?"

"Janice has left me for good this time. Please leave."

"Okay then, suit yourself, but I hope one day you'll realize that there's people out here in the world with real problems."

He turned around and walked back. He got his mail and parked the car beside the house. He got out, grabbed his rucksack and mail, and went inside. He put the rucksack beside his desk and went back to the kitchen.

He got out the dry oats and bottle of fish oil and mixed them inside the lidded jar and set it in the window sill. He fed the cat and washed his hands and went to his desk. He got out the essay and sat down. "Moonshine is the devil's handiwork," he whispered as he read the title.

He grabbed a pen and started reading the essay but stopped when he was halfway through the second paragraph. He wrote some arbitrary words in the margins, underlined a random sentence, and sat it aside. He tried to read the chapter on current events but ended up shaking his head at the prosaic poppycock. Then he got up and started gathering things for the next day.

He carried his rucksack to the kitchen door and filled up the canteen and put it inside the top flap. He washed his hands and went outside. He walked around to the basement door and disappeared inside. He came back out dragging the old canoe with one hand and carrying his paddle with the other. He leaned the canoe up against the side of the house and sat the paddle on top of it. He wiped the sweat off his face and looked at his watch. I have the rest of the day, he thought. He went back inside and changed his shoes and closed the house up. He went back out the door and took off walking.

He went down through the side yard to a small grove of poplar trees. He threaded his way through them and after a mile he came out on an old logging road shining with flakes of mica. He followed the road until he came upon the high tension power lines. He turned to the left and waded through a sea of waist high broomsedge frightening up buntings with every step he took. He stopped when he came upon an abandoned service road and looked around at the ground. He saw the tracks of deer and raccoons going through the moist red clay dirt. He decided to follow them but after a hundred yards he found himself lost in a thicket of rhododendrons. He worked his way through it until he was standing in a narrow opening on top of a small flat ridge. He looked around and recoiled when he saw that he was standing in the middle of a graveyard. Most of the gravestones were weathered beyond reading and a few of them were broken off and missing.

He eased down the line of markers trying to count them and read their names. He stopped at the end stone and read its weathered slate rock face. "Wilhelm Zimmerman," he whispered, "born nineteen hundred and eight but no date of death." He must be dead by now, he thought.

A branch snapped off behind him destroying the reverie and quietude of the little meadow. He whirled around but didn't see anything of concern. He listened and heard the faint whisper of the wind as it moved along through the boughs of the forest trees. He blinked a time or two and then retraced his steps back to his house as quickly as possible.

That night in bed he couldn't recall the event with any real clarity but it bothered him.

13

The next morning, after he had breakfast, he donned his rucksack and went outside. The air was warm and a slight zephyr stirred as he walked to the side of the house and flipped the canoe rightside up. He put his pack and paddle inside and started slowly dragging it down through the yard. He stopped at the end of his driveway to let a car by before continuing on across the road and down the hill toward the cove.

When he got to the riprap he pushed the canoe down into the water and started a careful descent through the rocks with his feet nimbly searching for places to step. He felt water sloshing against his ankles and turned around and took one big step into the cool shindeep water and smiled. He stepped over the gunwale, got in the lone seat, and commenced paddling.

There was a small chop to the water and the air smelled of campfire smoke as he paddled out of the cove. He heard Carolina wrens singing in the trees on the far shore and a big fish jumped on the starboard side of the canoe as he drew near the main channel of the lake. After he got there he sat the paddle aside and rode the natural movement of the water for half a mile. When he reached the bridge he retook the paddle and headed for a sandy shore on the port side.

He ran the nose of the canoe onto the beach and hopped out. He walked a few steps and picked up a sepia colored piece of driftwood that was curved like a boomerang. He turned back toward the lake and slung it with all his might. The piece of driftwood sailed in the air for a good distance before hitting a buoy and careening back into the water with a low thunk. He shrugged his shoulders and walked back to the canoe and stepped inside. He pushed himself off the sand with the paddle, sat down, and reverse stroked until he was almost back in the channel. Then he looked around him for any passing boats and started paddling toward Irish Creek.

He got there when the sun was high in the sky but the air was still pleasant and breezy. He ran the canoe aground next to the mouth of the creek and stepped out onto the small pebbled beach. He tossed the paddle inside and drug the canoe through some weeds and into a laurel thicket. He shouldered the rucksack and retraced his steps back to the mouth of the creek. He stopped when he got there and looked down at a small asymmetrical grouping of cairns. He nudged one of them over with the toe of his shoe and took off walking beside the shaded waterway.

After several miles he came upon an old dairy farm that had been converted into a hipster honkey-tonk. He slowed down and watched as the besotted bedlamites and ran back and forth in the pastureland like ancient and wild heathens. He looked up at the sky and signed and continued on. A short distance later he came upon the Irish Creek bridge. He stood there in the shade of the bridge and had a few sips of water from his canteen as he watched the ceaseless flow of the cool water. His mind started to drift away into a trance but a loud car passing overhead frightened him out of it. He wiped the sweat from his forehead, put his canteen up, and started up a small incline away from the creek.

He worked his way through a stand of poplar trees until he was standing at the edge of a small cow pasture without any discernible fencing. The heifers watched him with hushed indifference and didn't move as he took off in a fast trot for the woodline at the end of the field.

When he had gone several yards into the woods he stopped and sat down on an ashen colored rock and pulled his canteen back out. He had a swig of water and looked toward the western sky. Tenebrous clouds had formed near the mountains but showed no signs of advancing. He sat there until he heard a man's stout voice back in the pasture. Then he put his canteen back inside his rucksack and started walking again.

He went on, going through swales of sawbriars and thick underbrush until he came upon the placards that marked the property line of the park service. He went past the boundary and came upon a man in a hardhat peering through a metal box on a tripod. Catawba studied the man for a minute and then spoke.

"May I ask what you're doing?"

75

"Using a theodolite," the man replied dryly.

"Of course you are and what is a theodolite?"

"Surveying tool."

He took off walking again to the right of the man. He slowed down a hundred yards off and looked back. Then he sighed and directed his steps back toward the lake. When he got there he sat down on the red clay bank and recinched his laces and downed more water. He watched the fishermen trolling the far shore casting and reeling their lines and talking to one another in hushed voices. He put his canteen away after he stopped sweating and stood up and started walking back toward Irish Creek at a fast pace. As he drew close to the mouth of the creek he noticed Ranger Lowell standing on a large lichened rock. He slowed his pace and went over to him.

"Lowell, what are you doing out here today?"

"Just patrolling for code violations. What are you doing on this side of the lake?"

"My normal life. Some days I paddle over here and hike beside Irish Creek for a bit and then turn around and head back, but sometimes I just sit down in the woods and think. Today was a little bit of both I guess. Hey, I ran into a man who said he was surveying the land but he was out in the middle of the woods. I didn't say anything though. I just kept on walking."

"I know exactly what you're talking about," Lowell responded shyly. "The park service is getting ready to clearcut a large swath of forest for a road and educational center."

"Educational center? I thought the forest was the education, not a building. What in the world do they need that for?"

"They think we need a place to showcase nature exhibits and have classrooms," he replied as he took off his range hat. "But what do I know? I'm not in charge of anything,"

"What are they going to do with classrooms? I mean what are they going to teach?"

"Shit," Lowell muttered, "they want us to teach kids how to be nice to nature and not rape the land but you see what they are doing. Our natural resources and wilderness areas are managed by people who sit in offices many miles away and those people couldn't walk through the woods without a satellite phone and three trail guides."

"Lowell, I'm going home now. You don't want me to call in tomorrow and come over here and burn this place down."

Lowell said something else but Catawba didn't care to stop and listen. He went over to the laurel thicket and got out his canoe. He tossed his stuff inside and pulled it down into the lake. He climbed over the gunwale, picked up the paddle, and started paddling back towards home.

He got back to the cove after suppertime. He climbed out as soon as the nose of the canoe hit the bank. He grabbed the front handle and began pulling it up the hill with celerity. He stopped at the edge of the road to let a truck go by and get his mail. Then he went on, across the road, and up through the grass of his yard. He propped the canoe and paddle up against the side of the house and headed for the backdoor. He dropped his rucksack as soon as he got inside the kitchen and poured himself a big glass of ice cold water and went out onto the front porch. He leaned up against a column and stood there until dark peering out at the abyss.

14

The next morning he was sitting beside his bicycle when Vance came through the parking lot. He got up, grabbed his rucksack, and walked over to the truck. He put his pack in the toolbox, opened the door, and climbed in. Vance had a cigarette in his mouth and his aviators were on the dash in front of him. He didn't say anything as they drove away from the office.

"Anything happen at the park while I was off?" Catawba asked after they had gone a mile.

"I got in trouble."

"What did you get in trouble for?"

"Some asshole turned me into Mooseberg for staring at the women on the beach. But how would they know that? They can't see my eyes when I've got my shades on."

"That sounds horrible dude. Maybe you should get some different sunglasses, or better yet, you could stop acting like a damn degenerate."

Vance grunted, white knuckled the steering wheel, and pushed the gas pedal to the floorboard. Catawba closed his eyes and braced himself against the dashboard and door as the truck picked up speed. They pulled up in front of the bathhouse and Vance got out of the truck in a dead run. He went to the janitor's closet and flung the door open. Then he checked both sides of the bathhouse and motioned for Catawba to get out. He did what he was told and walked to the closet and got the cleaning cart out.

"I tell you what little buddy," Vance said angrily, "I'm going to let you spread your wings and fly today. Since you're so intelligent I'm going to let you knock out the entire campground while I go to the group picnic area."

"Thank you for the opportunity sir," Catawba replied as he took off pushing the cart towards the men's side.

He didn't look around to see it but he heard the squealing of truck tires as he opened the door and pulled the cart in. He got the broom out and started sweeping but stopped when he heard water trickling from the back shower stall. He leaned the broom up against the wall and walked over and pulled the curtain back to find a man lying there on the tile floor in a speedo. The man had glassy eyes and heavy breathing and behind his head was a half gallon bottle of gas station rotgut. Catawba kicked him in the ribs with the toe of his shoe. The man grunted and rolled over onto his side. Catawba stepped over him and got the empty bottle and took it to the trashcan and threw it away. He came back and kicked the man a few more times until he finally rolled over onto his back and looked up at him.

"I'll be ready in a jiff there chief. Lickety split."

Catawba nodded and went out. He pulled the shower curtain closed and went to the cleaning cart. He walked back over and hung up the OUT OF ORDER sign. Then he went on and finished cleaning the bathhouse and never thought about it again.

78

After he put the cleaning cart back in the closet he grabbed a few trash bags and a trash picker. He walked outside the closet, shut the door, and took off for the campsites.

He walked to the trashcan by the first site and raised the lid. Someone had shoved a broken plastic cooler inside of it and sat the lid back on top. He tried to yank it out but it wouldn't budge. He studied the problem for a minute but then he lost interest and walked on to the next can. He changed the bag and sat it on the ground. He picked up the small pieces of litter strewn on the ground and pitched them into the can. He heard something and turned around to see a man with a mullet standing there. He was drinking a beer and watching his movements.

"Yes sir, how may I help you?"

"I just wanted to say that this is the nicest place I have ever been and I've been all the way to Florida twice in my life."

"Thank you very much. As a member of the park service I guarantee you that your happiness is what we strive for on a daily basis."

"Jackass," the man yelled as he stormed off.

He stood there for several minutes and thought about the entirety of his life. Then he guffawed loudly and continued on his route.

When he got to the last campsite he saw a large family of large people sitting around a raging inferno. He changed the trash bag and picked up the little specks of trash around the can. He started to walk off but stopped and looked back at the family and spoke.

"Do you guys know that it's June and the temperature is supposed to be ninety-five degrees today?"

"Yes," yelled the family patriarch.

"Then why the bonfire?"

"You can't go camping without a fire. That wouldn't be American," the man yelled back even louder.

Catawba looked at the family's sweat soaked clothing, shrugged, and started walking back. He went along slowly, looking at the campers and their campsites. Some waved to him while others turned their back on him.

Vance met him at the halfway point of the service road. They circled back and collected the bags and headed for the dumpsters. They unloaded the trash together, Vance as silent as stone and Catawba not looking his way. Then they climbed back in the truck and drove to the maintenance shed on the hill.

The sprawling parking lot of the maintenance facility was filled with beat up trucks, rotting wood beams, signs from various epochs, fire fighting equipment, grading equipment, neglected lawn mowers, rock and sand piles, an above ground gas tank of dubious safety, and the personal vehicles of park staff.

Lenny was sitting outside in a metal folding chair with a pocket knife hacking away at a piece of wood when they came around the corner. He stood up and wiped the wood chips off his big belly as the truck parked.

"Get your rucksack," Vance said loudly as he got out.

"Okay," he replied.

He climbed out and got his rucksack. He shouldered it as he took off after him.

"Hey Lenny," Vance said unctuously, "I'm training Catawba today. I thought it would be a good time for him to learn all about trailwork since it's Friday and the park is slow."

"Proud to have you," Lenny said with a smile.

He looked at Lenny and around the parking lot as Vance got back in the truck and sped away. Lenny walked up to him and extended his hand.

"What?" Catawba asked as they shook hands firmly.

"It is just so rare that I have any company up here. They seem to forget that it takes a lot of effort to keep this park running at high efficiency. I maintain the entire park and I'm also in charge of all the safety protocols. Now, I don't take a lunch break. I work through it everyday so I can leave early. Do you have water?"

"I have some in my pack," he replied meekly.

"That's good. Now you go in the shed over there and grab a shovel and pickaxe and set them outside the door," Lenny said.

Catawba walked into the shed and got the tools out and shut the door. He turned around but Lenny had disappeared. He leaned the tools against the shed and got his canteen out and had a drink of water. He heard the straining of machinery and looked to his right to see a bulldozer creeping toward a large pile of rocks. It scooped up a bucketful of stones and drove to the end of the parking lot and dumped them inside the bed of an old dump truck. Then the bulldozer cut off and Lenny got out and walked over to him.

"I'm going to go get you some safety equipment from the park office. I'll be right back," he said.

Catawba nodded and Lenny walked over to his park truck and drove away. He stood there listening but heard nothing except the chirping of distant birds. He took his rucksack off and got out the lidded jar with the swollen oats. He uncapped it and smelled. He winced and held it out in front of him as he dashed over to Quincey's wagon. He looked around for a second and started sprinkling the noxious concoction in the gravel around the car. Then he slung a liberal amount of oats under the front bumper and laughed. He dumped the remainder of the jar in the tall weeds behind the rear hatch and walked back to put up the evidence.

When Lenny came sailing around the corner he was standing next to the shed examining the tools. Lenny got out and motioned for him.

"Take your pack off and toss it in the dumptruck. Toss the tools in too and when you get done I'll have your safety gear ready," Lenny said loudly.

He got the tools and took them to the truck. He tossed them in along with his rucksack. He turned around to see a small mountain of brightly colored safety equipment on the ground at Lenny's feet. He walked up to it and stopped.

"How many people is that for?"

"Just you. Now, I would help you too but I'm on light duty. I would hate to reinjure my back."

"I see," Catawba replied.

He reached down and started picking up various items and putting them on. He put on nylon safety chaps, a back brace, a Dayglo yellow safety vest, triple layered gloves, safety goggles, a hardhat, and sub-zero thermal rated earmuffs. When he got done he looked at Lenny through the scratched goggles and shook his head.

"How am I supposed to work in all of this without having a heat stroke?"

"You have water and I can run and get you some more," Lenny replied.

"Okay then. Let's go," Catawba said as he walked towards the truck.

They climbed into the cab of the old dumptruck and buckled up. Lenny turned the radio on and cranked up the volume. Then he backed up and left the maintenance shed parking lot.

Catawba braced himself as Lenny dashed around the park roads at twice the government mandated speed. Lenny would look over as he drove along and try to yell over the radio. Catawba kept nodding at his loud proclamations and pointing at him to look back at the road.

He drove to the park gate and cut out onto the main highway. They went over a handful of hills and then he slammed on the brakes. The truck stopped In the middle of the road with a cloud of rock dust. He looked to his right for a moment and then eased off the road and started down an embankment choked with pokeberry bushes and juvenile pine trees. Lenny gunned the engine and Catawba closed his eyes and they bounced out on a deserted trail. He opened his eyes up and reached over and turned down the radio.

"What's this trail?"

"This is the old Deer Dance Circle. We haven't used it for years. I got the park service to close it for safety reasons. Besides, I never have enough time to work on the trails."

He drove towards a small promontory and slammed on the brakes. He told Catawba to get out and sit his pack and tools beside the trail. He did what he was instructed to do and then he stepped behind a large oak tree. Lenny yelled something indecipherable and the dump bed lifted into the air causing an avalanche of rocks.

He got out and slammed the door and walked around to Catawba and motioned for him to follow. They took off walking slowly down the trail together with Lenny studying the ground between steps. He stopped after a hundred paces and looked up at Catawba.

"I need you to dig a ditch across the trail. It's for the prevention of erosion. The entire landmass of North America is slowly being destroyed by rainfall. I read it in an email."

"Why here?" he asked as he looked around.

"We have to start somewhere and this is as good a place as any. Go get your tools and I'll make you a mark."

Catawba walked back and picked up the shovel and pickaxe. He turned around to see Lenny making a line with the heel of his boot. He walked back over to him and tossed the tools down on the ground.

"Say Lenny, shouldn't we have brought a wheelbarrow since you dumped the rocks a hundred yards away?"

"Can't do it. You are not certified with the government when it comes to the usage of wheelbarrows. Now we could send you to a seminar but it wo…"

Catawba waved at him to stop. He grabbed the pickaxe and started swinging. Underneath the thin layer of topsoil he hit solid granite. He would swing and the pickaxe would make sparks every time it struck the rock face. Finally he stopped and wiped the deluge of sweat off his face. He looked around to see Lenny walking his way with his rucksack.

"Here you go little buddy," Lenny said merrily.

"Thanks."

Catawba grabbed his pack and sat it on the ground and dug his canteen out. He swallowed all the water in once pronounced gulp and wiped his mouth with the palm of his glove and looked over at Lenny.

"Now what?"

"What do you mean?"

"I mean what do you want me to do since I hit this big granite rock?"

"Oh that. Yes. Well. Just move a couple of feet over and try again. Make a straight line that goes across the trail. Just imagine a rain shower in the springtime and try to think about the flow of water. Speaking of water, I'm going to run up to the maintenance shed and get you some."

83

Catawba watched him walk back to the truck and climb inside. He cranked the engine and backed up around the rockpile before disappear ing from the direction from which they came. He shook his head in aggravation and stripped off all the safety gear as the sweat came out of every pore and the day grew hotter. He looked at his watch and hurried off to a large pine tree off in the woods. He laid down on the moist pine needles and started fanning himself.

After an hour passed, and the perspiration had subsided, he got up and dusted the needles off his body. He walked back to the trail and looked around but found nothing of concern. He headed on down the trail listening to the singing of unknown and unseen birds. He stopped several times and tried to click his tongue to their cadences but none responded. He went around a big bend in the trail and found himself staring directly at the top of Ranger Quincey's safari hat. He was bent over at the waist and fumbling with a trail camera on a tripod. Catawba stood stockstill and waited for him to speak.

"Hey there buddy," Quincey said when he looked up. "What are you doing?"

"Lenny has me out here on a trail project. I'm waiting for him to get back with some water because I am parched. I thought this trail was a circle. I've never been on it before to tell you the truth."

"That's nice Catawba. I'm out here putting up trail cameras. I have to catalog all the American woodcocks that inhabit this zone of the park and it can be a difficult process especially in this heat."

"Is woodcock something you hunt?"

"Yes. It is one of my favorite hobbies. The meat is simply divine when you roast it the way I do. See, I am also a culinary expert with a special emphasis on..."

Catawba sighed and listened and listened and listened until at last Quincey stopped talking. Then he spoke.

"I take a special interest in polecats. Are there many of those in the park?"

"Tsk tsk Catawba. Polecat is a colloquial nickname for the skunk. It is only used by uninformed locals such as

84

yourself. Its scientific name is Mephitis Mephitis. They are omnivores and opportunistic feeders. They'll eat anything from bird seed to insects but they are drawn mostly by oily fish and putrid chicken. It takes a skunk up to fourteen days to recharge after it sprays its noxious effluvium but I wouldn't worry too much about them, they only spray when they're cornered. Besides, the coyotes and foxes around here do a good job keeping the population thinned out."

"Wow Ranger Quincey, your knowledge of the natural world is quite impressive. You have inspired me to learn more about the environment. I have to get back to my project now," Catawba said as he slowly backed up. "Thank you for your time."

He turned around and took off in a slow jog back to the rock pile. He sat down when he got there and breathed a sigh of relief. An hour later he heard Lenny bouncing along the trail in the dumptruck. As soon as the truck stopped he picked everything up and tossed it into the back of the dump bed. He opened the door and climbed into the air conditioned cab and looked at Lenny.

"Where the hell were you at with the water?"

"I had to get caught on the paperwork. The park service requires all employees to sign out tools when they use them. As soon as I got the forms in good working order I got waylaid by Mooseberg. He said he needed me to respond to this email about the quarterly safety meeting and that meant calling the regional office..."

Catawba nodded in agreement as Lenny talked away and drove back up the hill through the brush. He jumped the truck back out onto the main highway and continued telling his story all the way back to the maintenance shed.

When the truck stopped Catawba got out and put the tools away while Lenny stayed in the air conditioned truck cab. Then he climbed back in and they drove down to the park office. He got out, grabbed his rucksack, and eased his tired body towards his bike. He turned around to wave goodbye but Lenny was already zig-zagging through pedestrians as he sped away. Then he kicked up the kickstand, climbed on the bike and started pedaling home with his muscles cramping from dehydration.

When he cut into his driveway he saw Don walking away from his house. He hopped off and started pushing the bike up the driveway by the handlebars.

"Hey there neighbor. I was just looking for you," Don said.

"Yeah. I just got done park rangering for the day. What do you want?"

"I was just seeing if you wanted to come have dinner with us."

"Where?"

"Up at the RV. We've got a five gallon bucket you can sit on and we can have a good smoke after we get done and then we can…"

"No thank you neighbor," he replied as he started up the porch steps with the bike, "see, some of us still have to work and pay taxes."

He leaned the bike up against one of the porch columns and went inside, slamming the door and leaving Don outside and alone. He dropped his rucksack in the hallway and walked to the thermostat and turned it all the way down. He went to the kitchen and chugged a big glass of water and stripped off all his clothes. Then he laid down on the cool linoleum floor and didn't move again until the wee hours of the morning.

15

The next day he found himself on public relations duty inside the park office. Mooseberg was sitting behind him at the superintendent's desk, doing paperwork and listening to the traffic on the radio. The morning started off slow with the usual phone calls about the usual things.

"Good Morning, Lake Linville Park. How may I help you?"

"Yeah, do you guys have camping there?"

"Yes sir. We have tent sites."

"Thank you."

"Good Morning, Lake Linville Park. How may I help you?"

"Do you guys have nature programs today?"

"Sir, nature is a never ending series of chemical and geological processes that stretches back billions of years to the time of single celled organisms. Now, I recently read a book about plate tectonics and it said...hello?"

"Lake Linville Park. Catawba Fox speaking. How may I help you?"

"Yes sir, are there any fish in the lake that a man can catch?"

"What do you mean?"

"Will they bite my hook?"

"Sir, I am not knowledgeable when it comes to the psychology of freshwater game. I do see people carrying fishing poles when I am outside walking around but their intentions are uncertain."

"Well shucks, I might head on to the ocean then."

"It's a free country. Godspeed and good luck to all your future endeavors."

"Hey Superintendent Mooseberg," he said loudly as he swiveled around in the office chair, "I think I've found my niche."

"Don't get too comfortable Catawba ," he responded, "this is only temporary. I think I'm going to assign you beach duty for the rest of the summer,"

"What does that consist of?"

"You'll stand down there on the beach and watch for people breaking the rules or swimming outside the roped off area."

"Can I go swimming too since it is so wretchedly hot?"

"My god man," he said as he got up and walked to the door of his office. "I want you to take this and don't say that I never gave you anything."

Mooseberg dug around in the pocket of his wool ranger pants and brought a small trinket and tossed it at him. He caught it in midair and examined it and discovered that it was a plastic orange lifeguard whistle on a shoestring. He slid it down into his back pocket and cleared his throat.

"Um, thank you sir. But what do you want me to do when it gets super hot down there? There isn't a tree down there at that beach."

"Damn it man," Mooseberg bellowed. "This place doesn't exist to serve you. Just drink a bottle of water and fan yourself with your empty hand."

"Okay."

"And Catawba, one more thing while I have it on my mind."

"Yes sir?"

"Stop running off into the woods to bother Quincey. The taxpayers are lucky to have such a national treasure working for them."

He let it go and didn't say anything more about it that morning. At noon he got out his lunch and ate in silence as he looked out the office window. The parking lot was starting to fill up and the various park staff filed in and out the backdoor in quick succession. Ranger Lansing came in and got a handful of brochures, Lenny came in and rooted around in a file cabinet, Vance came in and told a handful of lies about his extraordinary escapades in the park service, and finally Ranger Quincey stepped inside for a brief minute to pour out some wilderness word salad.

Around two o'clock the phone calls reached a fever pitch. He swiveled around in the chair and looked at Mooseberg . He was walking into the radio handset oblivious to the world around him. He eased back around and reached under the desk and unplugged the cord going into the phone jack. He turned back around to see Mooseberg high stepping it out of his office toward him.

"Catawba, Vance just radioed in a fire. You wait right here and don't move while I go check it out."

"Don't worry sir, I'll make you proud."

He sat there without moving while Mooseberg darted out the backdoor. Then he spun around in the chair and watched out the window as Mooseberg went to his park truck and left. He smiled as he leaned forward, unzipped the top of the rucksack and brought out the jar with the fish juice and oats.

He stood up and walked to the backdoor and disappeared outside. He walked down the handful of steps slowly, looking back and forth to see if anybody was watching him.

When he reached the bottom he knelt down and studied the leaves and dirt that lead up to the cavernous area under the steps. There was a very pronounced set of five toed tracks that went back and forth from the darkness. He uncapped the jar, laid down on his stomach, and flung the contents under the steps. Then he stood up, looked around, and hurried back inside the office.

An hour later Mooseberg came back to the office. He walked in the backdoor and removed his ranger hat and started fanning himself.

"I am going to tell you right now Catawba," he said with sheer joy, "if you ever want to be anything in this world you have to be like Vance. He just kept the whole shebang from going up in flames. Quick thinking like that is hard to come by these days. I am going to make sure he gets his name in the newspaper and a letter personally signed by all the top brass in the park service."

"But what about me?"

"What do you mean? You haven't done anything of value since you've been here."

"I ride my bike to work. Shouldn't I get a plaque for environmental stewardship or something?"

"Nonsense. Besides, you don't even wear a government approved helmet and I could write you a ticket just for that. Now sit there and look busy until you get off."

"Yes sir," he replied.

When the time came he gathered up his things and snuck out the backdoor. He climbed on the bicycle and pedaled home as the sun beat down on him.

16

The next morning he found himself standing in the grassy field next to the parking lot. A makeshift stage had been built and the stage was overflowing with all the head honchos from the capital. Vance was standing in the center of it all grinning as the regional director for the park service pinned a tawdry on his chest. Catawba shook his head and smiled at the pageantry.

At the conclusion of the pinning ceremony the regional director was offered a bullhorn, which he gladly took, and then used to deliver a tedious forty-five minute speech about the benevolence of humanity and the best traditions of the park service. Vance glowed and Mooseberg grew misty as the superlatives flowed forth from the director's mouth. The other staff members were away so the speech fell upon the ears of a random group of granola addicts and fanny packed senior citizens. The service ended with a stirring tribute to the flag and excessive hand shaking. Catawba rolled his eyes and waited when he saw Vance heading his way.

"Did you see that Catawba? The regional director himself said I was the epitome of perfection."

"That's nice. So what went down?"

"You saw it with your own eyes. You were standing right here."

"No with the fire."

"Oh that," he said as he lit a smoke. "I was driving along and came upon a ditch that was smoldering at the edge of the forest. I radioed it in and then took off for the maintenance shed and got a bucket of water and a fire rake. I drove back and just happened to be extinguishing the last ember when Mooseberg drove up. If there's one thing I know it's that some people are just in the right place at the right time. You take care now," he said as he slapped Catawba's shoulder. "They gave me the rest of the day off."

Catawba watched him walk away and chuckled. Then he headed back to the park office. He went inside and got a drink of water from the fountain. He turned around and found himself chest to chest with Mooseburg.

"Catawba, did you unplug the phone?"

"I have no clue what you are talking about sir."

"Go right to my office and sit down."

He didn't utter a sound as he walked into the superintendent's office and sat down in the chair. Mooseberg followed behind him and handed him an already typed out piece of paper off the desk. He read it quickly and signed without protest.

"One more write up and you're out the door," Mooseberg said as he sat down. "You may live here at the lake but you won't work here at the park as long as I have anything to do with it."

"Well what do you want me to do for the rest of the day?"

"Catawba, just go out there to that desk and answer the phone. I want to keep my eye on you today but from here on out you'll be on the beach."

He got up and went over to the desk next to the window and sat down and resigned himself to a day of tedium and malaise.

When lunchtime came he dug a pear out of his rucksack and went outside. He walked to the other end of the parking lot and sat down under a maple tree. He sat there in silence, watching as throngs of people marched about with enough picnic stuff to feed a small army. After a while he looked down at his watch and got up and dusted off his backside. He took off walking toward the office but stopped when he saw a man slinging glass beer bottles in the woods. He shook with anger and marched inside to his boss.

"Hey Superintendent Mooseberg, some guy just slung his trash in the woods."

"Well what do you want me to do about it?"

"I don't know, can't you give him a ticket or something?"

"Catawba, let me make the decisions. Do you have any idea how much paperwork would be involved in that?"

He turned around and walked back over to the desk at the window. He sat down and began answering phone calls with mordacious brevity. Ranger Lansing came in a short time later and asked Mooseberg to go with him on foot patrol. Catawba waited until they were gone before bringing out the lidded jar. He went outside, did the deed, and came back in. Mooseberg came back an hour later. He took off his ranger hat and sat it on top of the file cabinet. He gave Catawba a hostile glance before going back to his office.

When the time came for him to get off he stood up and shouldered his rucksack. He told Mooseberg farewell and went outside without waiting for a reply.

17

The next day was Monday and he slept till noon. He rolled out of bed, fed the cat, and made himself a cup of strong coffee. He walked out onto the porch and stood there sipping away at his brew as he listened to the sounds of birds emanating from the treetops around him. He smelled a faint wisp of smoke and walked to the edge of the porch and looked over at his neighbor's RV.

Janice was walking around with a small metal can dousing the young weeds with gas and Don followed behind her striking kitchen matches as he went. The tiny pieces of foliage would shrivel up when the match touched them releasing a small plume of chemical laden smoke. Catawba laughed and went back inside.

After he ate lunch he tried to get on the internet but there was no connection. He checked the cord between his ancient laptop and the modem but found nothing wrong. He got on the phone and called the internet service provider. Then he sat down at the table and waited. A recorded voice came on the line and told him that because of increased call volume the wait would be ten minutes. I can do that, he thought.

An hour and a half later a man answered the phone and told him to turn his computer off and cut it back on. He followed the instructions but nothing happened. He went to speak again but the man had already hung up. He slammed the phone down on the table and stood up. He snatched up his laptop, grabbed his keys, and took off out the backdoor for his car.

The roads were empty as he sped down the main highway towards town. After the first set of traffic lights he cut off into the Fonta Flora Heights shopping center and drove down to the computer store. He got out and hurried inside with the laptop in the crook of his arm.

The store was brightly lit and the sales associates sauntered about like emotionless automatons. He walked to the middle of the store and turned down the computer aisle and began looking at the desktops and laptops methodically. The King's English is no more, he thought as he read the laminated placards. He turned around to see that he was being tailed by an associate.

"May I help you sir?"

"Uh yes, I think my laptop is dead. I need a new one," he replied as he handed it over.

"Are you a gamer?"

"Not really. I mean I played right field in little league but that was when I was kid."

"I see sir, do you have any storage or graphic requirements?"

"Uh," he replied as he scratched his jaw, "I need a laptop I can use for writing and to go on the internet with."

"I see sir, I think I know what you are after. Please follow me."

Catawba followed him down to the end of the aisle. The man put the laptop in an empty bin and unlocked the display case. He handed him a new laptop in a box and disappeared. He came back shortly thereafter and sat a mountain of cords on top of the box.

"Is this thing hard to connect?"

"Not at all sir, you'll find that the instructions are very clear. They're written in the language of the common man," the associate said before walking away.

He stood there for a moment pondering the experience before turning around and taking his items up to the cashier. The cashier scanned the items and started bagging them up but stopped when a loud voice came from behind him.

"Fox? Catawba Fox?"

He turned around to see a lanky man with wavy hair rushing toward him. The man held out his hand and Catawba shook it as he searched his brain for the man's name.

"Don't you remember me? We were in the same computer class back in high school."

"Of course I do," he replied hesitantly. "How've you been?"

"My life is beyond words. That class changed my life. I realized the path to a brighter future and better tomorrow is technology. So I went on and studied computer science at a college up north. And guess what?"

"What?"

"I'm going to be a teacher here at the state school of robotics they're building. I'm married and I have three beautiful kids in private school who are at the top of their classes. I just bought a house in a gated community and just wow," the man said with a smile. "So what are you doing with yourself these days? I remember you used to gush about the world and you were so creative."

"Well you wouldn't believe it if I told you, but I'm researching wildlife psychology for the park service. And when I'm not doing that I'm volunteering at the public library. Just doing my part to eradicate rural illiteracy and be a model citizen. Say buddy, let me pay and I'll talk to you some more outside."

The man said something inaudible and slapped Catawba's shoulder. He headed for the door and Catawba turned back to the cashier. He signed the receipt slip quickly and she put it in the till.

"Hey miss," he said in a whisper, "do you have a backdoor I can use?"

"Go through the double doors in the back and head out the metal door at the loading dock. If that weirdo darts back in here I'll tell him you went to the bathroom."

"Thank you kindly," he replied as he grabbed up his bags.

He sprinted across the store, through the double doors, and past a napping stocker. He went out the metal door and stood on the loading dock trying to catch his breath. Then he sat down on the concrete loading dock and looked out at the haggard trees on top of the ridge and waited.

After an hour he got up and walked around to the front of the store with his bags. The man was gone but the heat rising from the asphalt felt miserable. He walked over to his car, put the bags in the passenger's seat, and left for home.

When he walked through the backdoor he went to the kitchen table and sat everything down. He unboxed the new laptop and took the plastic off of it. He picked up the box and shook it but the directions were not to be found. He sat the box down and studied the multicolored cords. He rubbed his chin and thought for a second and then smiled. He put everything back in its proper packaging and picked up the bags and headed outside. He walked quickly across the driveway to the RV and knocked on the door. It opened as if it were spring loaded and Don stepped outside with a big smile on his face.

"What's going on today neighbor?"

"I'm sorry about the other day Don. I'd just got off from work and I was beat."

"It's alright. I figured you were one of those tense people you see all the time on TV."

"The TV people?"

Don cocked his head sideways and looked at him like a bewildered canine. Catawba sat the bags on the ground, stepped back, and gestured at them with his hands.

"What's that?"

"Don, you guys gave me a gift basket when I first met you and I didn't even offer you anything in return. So, since you guys have turned out to be such great neighbors I decided to buy you a gift."

"What is it?"

"Look inside. It's a surprise but I think it will fit you to a tee."

He bent at the waist and picked up the bags. He started rifling inside and brought out the laptop box and studied it for a second. Then his face lit up and he looked at Catawba.

"I have always wanted one of these," he cried. "Hey Janice, come out here."

She emerged from inside and Don told her about it. She grew elated and gave Catawba a big and forceful hug. He pushed her off and took two steps back.

"Now you guys have fun with that and tell me how it works out for you."

Catawba turned around and took off in a rush for the house. He went inside and grabbed one of the kitchen chairs and carried it to his book shelf. He stepped up on it and grabbed his antique Royal Deluxe typewriter off the top shelf. He got down and carried it over to the desk and sat it atop the lacquered oak surface and blew the dust off the keys. He smiled as he walked back to get a ream of paper.

The next day he drove over to his grandfather's house. The old man was sitting out on the porch in a rocking chair watching a chubby teen mow the grass. He parked next to the sidewalk and got out. He walked up the steps and eased himself down in the wood slatted porch swing. After a few minutes he cleared his throat and his grandfather looked over at him.

"What is it?"

"Who's the kid mowing the grass?"

"That's the boy who lives two houses down. He gets my mail for me when it rains too. I'm going to start letting him cut the grass since you're always busy."

"Always busy? I always cut the grass. I call you everyday and come by several times a week to check on you."

"But I never know for sure when you're coming by. This will be better. He lives closer too," the old man replied.

"I live two miles away and you can call me anytime."

"The boy said he can fix my clock and windmill too. Did you ever get me that dog?"

Catawba stood up and walked to the far side of the porch. He leaned against the column and dug his fingernails into the chipping paint. He turned around to say something but his grandfather was already back watching the kid. He shook his head and walked off the porch and headed for the car.

18

The next morning he was sitting in class watching Professor Binetti as he shuffled through papers and talked. He told the class about the rhapsodic beauty of his childhood home in New England and his election to the vice-chairmanship at the National Society for Educational Excellence. Two of the students agreed in unison with every word he said until at last he grew serious and started the lecture.

"Okay class, today we are going to go over current events," he said with great enthusiasm. "Who amongst you reads the local newspaper?"

"Yes, yes, that is good," he said as searched around the room for hands.

Then his eyes settled on Catawba who sat motionless with his hands in his lap.

"I see we have a social nonconformist in our midst. So Catawba what is your hostility to the newspaper? Are you some political extremist who believes that the media is lying to the masses?"

"No sir, I just hate gentrification, and I do not want to hear about change, especially if getting a new fitness center means destroying a family run business or if getting a new outdoor adventure store means cutting down more trees to build more trails. And that's all the news around here seems to be, businesses and change that I don't remember anybody asking for."

"But that's progress. You can't stand in the way of progress can you?"

"Sir, everyone talks about progress but no one talks about what we're progressing towards. Besides, if the spirit of the community is destroyed then what was the point?"

"Do you watch the national news then?"

"Yes sir, I do watch that now. I think it is important to keep up with what is going on in the nation but not here. Besides, I don't live inside the city limits. I live out in the country which means I'm on the outside looking in."

"This sounds like a discussion in ethics and I am not a philosophy professor. So, since you don't read the newspaper I want you to go out into the city and write down what you see for class next week. Can you do that for me?"

"Sure," he responded loudly, "but I do not want to get in trouble if what I write about the world scares the living hell out of you."

"I promise you that in all my decades of teaching I've read it all. So don't worry young man."

Catawba nodded and Binetti went back to the lecture. He sat there for a few seconds then he looked over at Nevena. Her face was beet red and the veins on her forehead pulsated with every heartbeat she took.

When the class adjourned he walked over and exchanged essays with Beth. He went back and shoved the paper inside his pack and yanked the zipper closed. He turned around to speak to Nevena but she was gone. He picked up his stuff and walked briskly out the door.

He went to his car, drove across town to the public library, and parked. He got out and took off walking down the shady sidewalk of South King Street. He went through the crosswalk and kept going under the branches of ornamental oak trees. He turned right at the next intersection and went down a gentrified street populated with cavalier baristas and mendicants who studied each other in standoffish displays. He got to a big intersection and pushed the crosswalk button on a big wrought iron dial clock. He looked to his right and saw a large assemblage of humanity facing the grassy purlieu of the old courthouse. When the light changed over he walked toward them with quick indifference.

As he drew near he saw that the century old trees on the courthouse lawn were spray painted orange. He stopped at the back of the crowd and tapped the shoulder of the man in front of him. The man turned around in a flash and looked at him.

"What's going on here?"

"They are going to cut down the trees next to the courthouse."

"Why? Why would they do such a thing? They've been here forever."

"They want to build a stage and bathrooms for a music venue. That's their reasoning or so the mayor said a few minutes ago."

"Which one is he? The mayor?"

"He's over there with the general contractor," the man said as he pointed towards a small knot of people. "The guy with the white hair and black suit."

Catawba looked that way to see the besuited mayor studying a large set of blueprints surrounded by a semicircle of other city officials in gilded attire.

He took off through the mass of people but when he got to the head of the crowd he found that the way was barricaded with fencing and guarded by adipose policemen. He turned around and threaded his way back through the crowd and started running back towards his car. He stopped when he got to the steps of the library and sat down and tried to catch his breath. He heard a chainsaw crank up, followed shortly thereafter by the thump, thump, thump of the tree trunks smacking the ground. The cords in his neck seized up and he staggered up to his feet and headed for the car.

He drove up the highway with a devil-may-care attitude, speeding and passing cars in every straightaway he entered. He slid into his driveway and got out. He stormed inside the house and sat down in front of his typewriter. He readied a piece of paper and rested his fingers on the keys. Then he exhaled deeply, closed his eyes, and started typing…

Massa Damnata

We watched them go past with their shiny wagon. Him sitting there in the shopkeeper's best raiments studying the sun against the sky trailed by a retinue of wild eyed fanatics all bedecked in their chiseled fineries. We beseeched them to stop but they marched on. They said they were missionaries heading toward the setting sun to evangelize the heathen, but we knew they were not missionaries, we knew they were false prophets.

We went back to the fields after they passed and returned to our domiciles after the setting of the sun. Each man shopworn in life and soul awaiting the christian verdict.

We awoke in the middle of the pitchblack night to the sound of screams. Once mustered outside we discovered that the previous day's pilgrims had been hacked to death and their wagon was nothing more than a makeshift bonfire.

In the days that followed no account given was the same and no explanation allowed was satisfactory. We heard rumors and whisperings in all corners of the countryside but once inspected they vanished like vapor in the wind.

A fortnight removed from the event we carried creekstone to the town cemetery and a few of the masons made mortar. Monuments were erected at the heads of the gravesites and the church deacons scratched crosses on the capstones.

The town constable checked his timepiece and asked if any amongst us had a word to say for the departed souls interred beneath our feet, but he was met with only silence and the twittering of birds in the distant fields. We turned to go but stopped when a half crazed man emerged from the forest and came rushing through the crowd. He climbed to the top of the largest monument and raised his hands up toward the cerulean sky. He looked at us with eyes of cold implacability and smiled. A clap of thunder boomed behind him and with that he began a fiery homily about the footfalls of iniquity, the laughter of children, and how the disquieting march of concupiscence is leading the masses to Megiddo…

19

He got up Friday morning at sunrise and drove his car over to the park office. When he pulled into the parking lot he found the place deserted. He got out and went on his fishy constitutional to the back steps of the office. He did the deed and returned the jar to the floorboard of his car.

He was leaning against the information board when, like clockwork, Vance showed up in the park truck. He motioned for Catawba to get in but he shook his head. Vance got out of the truck and walked over to him.

"What's wrong? You didn't ride your bike today. Is everything okay?"

"Nothing is wrong. It's just too hot to ride my bike home when I get off. Oh yeah, and Mooseberg said that from now on I'm stationed on the beach. I thought I would flag you down and tell you before I went down there," he said calmly.

Vance tossed his burning cigarette onto the ground, hitched up his pants, and walked quickly back to the truck. He opened the door but yelled and then slammed it with all his might. He put his hands on his hips and looked at Catawba with malevolence.

"I'll tell you what you little shit," he said slowly but loudly, "I haven't spent thirty years swabbing toilets and battling forest fires for the park service just to have some snot nose ruin my life."

"What the hell Vance? Is that your retirement plan? Chain smoking on a beach and looking at women who wouldn't be caught dead with you?"

"I'll show you dead you mouthy little bastard."

Catawba spun around and took off running down the sidewalk beside the office with Vance in hot pursuit. He turned right and went down through the picnic area with Vance three steps behind him. Vance yelled and wheezed as Catawba cackled in full stride. They dashed through the grassy field before turning back into the parking lot. Catawba juked left and then headed back towards the park office. He kicked it into high gear as he headed for the end of the sidewalk. He jumped onto the trunk of a massive pine tree and clambered up the side of it until he was looking down at Vance.

"Ass clown. Ass clown. Ass Clown," Vance shouted as he jumped up and down.

He began pacing around the base of the tree with a near religious intensity. Catawba looked up and smiled as a park truck came sailing through the parking lot. The truck stopped in front of the office and Ranger Lansing and Lenny got out in unison and began walking toward the tree. Vance turned around in a flash but slumped down when he saw who it was. He took off for the office in a defeated gait with Lenny right behind him.

"What happened here? And get down from that tree," Lansing commanded.

He scurried down the tree trunk and stood in front of him. He began dusting himself off as he told his boss all about the incident.

"...and I kept telling him sir that this is not keeping with the best traditions of the park service," he said in closing.

"I'm going to have to tell Mooseberg about this. I just hope he's in a good mood today. Now go down to the water and stay away from Vance."

Catawba took off walking to the beach. He sat down on a large rock at the edge of the sand and watched the little minnows dart back and forth under the placid water. After a while he looked toward the office but he didn't see anyone heading his way.

As the morning marched on, the day grew hot. He got up and headed for the office to get a drink of water. He saw Mooseberg's vehicle parked out front as he ascended the steps. He took a deep breath, opened the door, and went inside. He heard typing coming from the superintendent's office but it stopped when the door closed behind him.

"Is that you Quincey?"

"No sir, it's me Catawba."

"Mr. Fox, will you come back to my office for a minute?"

"Yes sir."

He walked into the office and sat down in a chair. Mooseberg swiveled around and put his elbows on the top of the desk. He stared directly at Catawba who sat quietly looking around at the pictures on the walls.

"That's a nice one there," he said, pointing at a framed picture, "where was it taken at?"

"The southern tip of Lake Michigan."

"Seems nice. I bet they have a lot of ducks up there. "

"I wouldn't know. I never took the time to count them."

"Am I in trouble sir?"

"Mr. Fox, do you know the difference between mitigating and aggravating factors?"

"One is good and the other one is not so good right?"

"Yes, that's right. You have a bunch of aggravating factors on your record and nothing to mitigate them. You haven't even been here a month and you have been nothing but a headache. You need to do something to clean your slate and save your job. I know this is seasonal employment but I can terminate you with three write-ups or a call to the regional director. Now do you understand Mr. Fox?"

"Yes sir I do. I need to shine. I need to be more like Vance. I need to make the taxpayers proud. I need to be the standard bearer for all things wholesome and American. To be the torch in the midst of the incessant darkness that seeks to envelope the land. I need to..."

"Shut up," Mooseberg snapped, "and take your ass back to the beach."

He nodded and got up. He went to the fountain and had a drink of water before heading out the door. He went outside and walked back to the beach and sat down Indian style in the beige colored sand. He watched the kids playing while their parents napped in chairs. He stood up a few times and yelled at teenagers to get back inside the roped off area. An hour later he heard a voice from behind him.

"Hey Catawba."

He turned around to see Mooseberg watching him from the edge of the sand. He got up and walked over to him.

"What's wrong sir?"

"Are you not going to take a lunch break?"

"No sir, those days are done. Lenny taught me that a dedicated employee always works through lunch."

"Very good Mr. Fox, but I have my eye on you. I have to go run some errands so you'll be in charge of both the swimming area and picnic area for a little while. Quincey is out in the forest measuring trees and Lansing is on lake patrol in the boat. If you need someone just go to the office. Lowell is in there."

"Okay, I might go get another drink of water here in a little bit."

"That's fine but make it quick. The park staff is spread thin today."

He walked back to the edge of the water and stood. He waited a few seconds and glanced over his shoulder. He saw Mooseberg going up the pavement past the building. Then he turned around and headed straight for the park office. He walked up the back steps, opened the door, and went inside.

When the door shut Ranger Lowell swiveled around in the chair and looked at him.

"Yowzer, there's a lot of people out there."

"You can say that again."

"How many people come to Lake Linville Park in a normal year?"

"Let's see, I think the last time they did a count it was in the neighborhood of five hundred thousand people a year but when they get the new educational center built that number will double. More attractions equals more visitors and more visitors equals more funding."

"That doesn't sound very environmentally friendly sir."

"Funding is the name of the game, not nature."

"I've sort of figured that out already. Did you know they cut down the trees at the old courthouse and that they're clear cutting on the other side of the lake?"

"Yeah, I knew that was going to happen. They sent us a letter about it last year. Sucks doesn't it?"

"Yep, the enchanted land of my childhood is being destroyed in more ways than one and there is no way to level the playing field it seems."

"That's a fact. Anyway, what do you need? Is there something wrong down in the picnic area?"

"Nope. I just wanted to come inside and cool off and maybe get a drink of water. Do you think you could watch the swimming area for fifteen minutes?"

"Sure I will," he replied as he donned his ranger hat and headed for the door.

Lowell opened the door and disappeared outside. Catawba snuck to the window, fingered open the miniblinds, and saw him trotting towards the swimming area. He twisted the lock on the backdoor and ran to the front door and locked it too. He came back to the brochure rack, picked one up, and unfolded it as he walked quickly into Mooseberg's office. He turned on the computer and sat down in the superintendent's chair. He tapped his fingers on the top of the desk and waited.

When the desktop screen came up he took the mouse and clicked on the email icon. He clicked on compose and a blank box popped up. He read the bottom of the brochure and entered the park's official email address. He tabbed down to the subject box and typed: My experience at your picturesque park. He tabbed again and started typing the message...

To whom it may concern,

My name is Eleanor Kennedy and I am a lifelong enjoyer of maritime adventure. Recently, my fantastic husband and I decided to partake in one of the various aquatic activities you have listed on your website. We arrived last Saturday just as the sun began its quotidian duty of illuminating all things great and green. We put in our two person kayak near the swimming area and started paddling out toward the lake channel. As we drew near the first buoy a cyclonic wind descended down from a mountain pass and capsized our boat. We were both wearing Coast Guard approved personal flotation devices but alas my husband still floundered in the choppy water. I tried to swim to my beloved hubby but the wind pushed me toward the shore. I thought all was lost, but then, out of the corner of my eye, I saw a flaxen haired young man breast stroking through the water like a Bottlenose dolphin. He grabbed my husband around the waist and swam him back to shore. He pulled him out and onto the sand and then swam back out and got me too. My husband and I were rejoicing and weeping as he swam back out, yet again, to bring back our kayak. When he got back he flipped it upside down and made us sit on it while he administered triage and checked for wounds. I told him we were fine and thanked him for his heroic and praiseworthy actions. He nodded and told me that it was his humble duty as a dedicated public servant. I asked him his name and he told me. Now, I had a lot of water in my ears, but I think he said his name was either Freddy or Bobby or it could have been Catawba Fox but I'm not sure. It doesn't matter though because this young man certainly makes his presence known.
Thank you for your time,
Eleanor

He read it out loud, grinned, and hit send. Then he stood up and stretched and refolded the brochure. He put it back in the rack and got a drink of water and unlocked the backdoor. Ranger Lowell came back inside shortly thereafter and took his ranger off and tossed it on the desk.

"You weren't kidding about the people," he said loudly as he wiped the sweat off his forehead. "For a Friday afternoon it's quite busy. There seems to be a large family down there in the picnic area having a reunion and the kids in the swimming area are splashing up a storm. There must be a lot of people fishing on the shoreline because the entire outside smells like rancid fish. I didn't see much in the way of trash though, so I'd just let the evening shift deal with it."

"That sounds about right sir, but don't worry, I'll keep an eye on it. Thanks for giving me a breather," Catawba replied before going out the door.

He smiled as he walked down the back steps and headed for the swimming area. He sat down on a large rock at the edge of the water and started daydreaming. Children came up to him several times during the rest of his shift and asked him for help blowing up their floats. He obliged and yelled at them to be careful as they dashed away.

When his watch struck three he stood up and started a slow march to his car. As he walked past the park office he waved at the evening workers who stood in the breezeway waiting for their shift to start. He got to his car and started to open the door but froze when he felt a hand tapping his shoulder. He turned around to see Vance standing there in his aviator sunglasses.

"What do you want? I'm tired and I want to go home."

"Catawba, I want to apologize for my conduct earlier. That was not the type of conduct and professionalism that someone with my level of seniority should display. May I ask you a question?"

"Sure Vance."

"Why did you drive today instead of riding your bike?"

"Because it's just too hot for the bike. It's too hot for the rucksack. It's just too damn hot for anything."

"That makes sense, I guess. If you were properly certified, like me, you could have your very own park truck and ride around in the air conditioning."

"Thanks but no thanks. I think I'll forgo all that hoopla," he said as he turned around.

He climbed inside and shut the door and cranked the car and turned the air conditioning on full blast. He sat there for a while looking out across the grassy field toward the picnic area as the arctic air blew in his face. When he cooled off he put the car in gear and backed out of the space but then he stopped. He saw a furry black head peeking out from under the back steps of the office. The creature retreated when a small child screamed out near the swimming area. He put the car in drive and headed home with a devious smile on his face.

He pulled into his driveway to find that a large pile of wooden beams had been delivered to his neighbors property. He got out and walked over to inspect them. The beams were huge and notched out for each other and he ran his hand slowly along the top of them as he walked around. He looked up to see Janice coming out of the RV.

"That's our future home," she said happily.

"How do you guys plan on putting this thing together? These beams weigh at least a hundred pounds apiece."

"We put an ad in the local classifieds. We said we were looking for a couple of men with strong backs. I'm sure they'll start calling us any day now. Say Catawba, you could help us too when you're off."

"I would if I didn't have that loopy job for the park service. Let's talk about this more when it cools down some."

"That's fine," she replied.

He turned around and took a couple of steps but stopped when he heard the aluminum door slam behind him.

"Hey neighbor," Don called out, "want to come have a quick smoke with me? I want to tell you all about this website I found that says you can put geothermal heat in a log home."

"Nah, I'm good. I have to go home and shower and eat my dinner like a normal human being."

"Catawba this pot is medical grade and it was..."

He took off walking for his house and didn't respond. He went in through the backdoor and ripped off all his clothes and tossed them in the washing machine. He went to the bathroom and took a long shower. He hummed at the wall as the cool water ran over his parched skin. Then he hopped out and dried off and got dressed. He fed the cat and called his grandfather. He told him he would come over sometime Monday and that made the old man happy. Then he hung up the phone and got a big glass of water. He sipped the cold liquids slowly, looking out the kitchen window at the pine copse beyond the grass.

20

The next morning he got out of his car and took off walking toward the park office. He stopped a short distance away from the back steps and looked at the ground. Small ruts and divots were dug out and little mounds of black scat littered the area. He cocked his head sideways and listened to the chorus of critter sounds coming from the darkness beneath the steps. He smiled and started whistling a merry tune as he headed for the front door. He went inside the dark and deserted office and shut the door behind him and locked it. He walked over to the park service radio equipment and pulled the chair out and sat down. He picked up the corded microphone and pushed the talk button.

"Seasonal Employee Fox calling Ranger Quincey."

"Go ahead Fox. This is Quincey."

"Yes sir, I was just walking across the parking lot when I noticed an American woodcock hopping along the ground behind the backdoor of the office. The bird tried to fly away when I went up the back steps but it appeared to have a hurt wing. I just went outside to check on it and the poor creature appears to be trapped under the steps. Do you want me to attempt a rescue?"

"Stand down, Stand down I say," boomed Quincey's voice through the radio speaker. "Do not in any way try to intervene. I'm out on a trail but I will be there as soon as possible. You are not certified to deal with environmental emergencies of this magnitude. Quincey Out."

Catawba dropped the corded radio, stood up, and stretched. He went to the front door and disappeared outside. He walked down through the picnic area looking at the clean and empty sites. He turned left at the water and began walking alongside the lakeshore. He picked up a flat quartz rock and tried to skip it across the smooth water but it hit the surface with a ka-thunk and disappeared into the silt. He shrugged and walked out onto the beach where an older couple were sitting in the sand.

"Did you guys get here when the park opened?"

"Yes sir, we've been here since the front gates opened," the woman replied. "You have to get up bright and early if you want to get a jump on the heathens."

"I understand completely," he said as he trotted on through the sand.

He walked to the edge of the water and stopped. He looked down at his hikers and watched the slight motion of the water cresting against the toes of his shoes.

An hour later he saw a ranger walking quickly his way. He squinted but couldn't make out who it was until they got close and spoke.

"Catawba Fox," Ranger Lansing snapped, "I need you to meet me and Mooseburg in the basement right this minute. We have to discuss an incident that happened recently."

"I'm heading there now," he replied as he took off walking.

He passed by Lansing without saying another word. He got to the basement door and opened it up and went inside. There were three chairs sitting in a triangle with Mooseberg sitting in the far chair reading a piece of paper. Catawba walked to the first chair and sat down. Lansing closed the door, followed behind him, and sat down too.

"Okay," Mooseberg began, "we need to talk about a certain incident that happened recently at the park."

"Don't worry sir, Vance and I buried the hatchet."

"No Mr. Fox, that's not it. It has been brought to our attention that you have done a good deed that deserves recognition," Lansing said with a nod.

"Hmm, I wonder what it can be," Catawba said with a smile, "I am the same everyday and to everyone. I guess someone just finally noticed."

"Do you happen to know someone by the name of Eleanor Kennedy?"

"That name doesn't ring a bell sir."

"Mr. Fox, I want you to read this email that was sent to us by a park visitor."

Mooseberg passed him the paper and sat back and waited. Catawba studied the email for a moment and then looked up at the smiling faces of his bosses.

"Oh yeah guys," he began, "I had to swim out and help these kayakers who were having trouble. I didn't think much about it at the time but I guess I should have told someone. Is my slate clean now?"

"I want you to read aloud the sender's email address," Lansing said.

Catawba looked down at the paper and started to speak.

"Dumbass," Mooseberg snapped, "you sent that nonsense from my official government email address didn't you?"

"Sir, I am an idiot. Computer usage is not my strongest virtue."

"Of course you're an idiot. No one can do anything without proper certification. The world would descend into a hellish anarchy if it weren't for seminars and certifications and safety meetings. Now I think it's best if we..."

"If we do what?"

All three turned toward the door when they heard a high pitched scream come from outside. Catawba took off running for the door with Mooseberg and Lansing right behind him. He flung the door open to find an upturned safari hat and a noxious smell hanging in the air. He looked to his right and saw a trail of discarded park service attire heading downhill toward the lake. The trio took off together in a sprint for the water. When they got there they found Ranger Quincey bobbing up and down in the water thirty yards offshore.

"What happened?" Mooseberg asked loudly.

"That wasn't a woodcock Catawba. That was a skunk. There is an army of skunks under the back steps."

"The correct terminology is surfeit of skunks. But you were right about one thing though Quincey ."

"Huh? What? Huh?"

" Foxes do prey on skunks," Catawba yelled out with a smile.

"CATAWBA FOX YOU ARE FIRED," Mooseberg shouted at the top of his lungs. "I want you to take your ass home and never come back. Do you hear me?"

Catawba laughed, turned around, and walked briskly up the hill without a care in the world. He stopped at the back steps and listened but everything was quiet. He looked down at the ground and saw numerous skunk tracks leading off into the woods. He nodded his head and walked to his car and left.

He pulled up into his driveway and got out. Don and Janice were sitting outside with a bong in between them. He shut his car door and walked over to them.

"Next week," she said in drugged sluggishness, "there is a guy coming to help us put our log home together."

"That's right," Don chimed in. "I found his number on the back page of the Fonta Flora Gazette."

"I'm sure he'll be of the utmost quality then."

"Hey, do you want to help?" she asked.

"Yeah, I could pitch in a day or two. I think that would be the neighborly thing to do."

"Here," she said as she got up, "I have something for you."

She went inside the RV and came back out with a rolled up flag and handed it to him. He unrolled it and looked at it.

"And what is this?" he asked as he studied the strange symbols.

"That's a coat of arms. It's from the Netherlands. It's Dutch."

"Well, what do you want me to do with it? My ancestors weren't from there."

"Fly it on the front of your house. It'll make you look cultured. That's what we do. That's the reason we are always hanging up flags."

Catawba looked up at the RV and then back down at the two stoners staring at him. He sighed, tucked it under his arm, and carried it back to his house. He went inside, tossed it in a closet, and fed his cat. He made himself a sandwich and carried it to his desk. He sat down and ate slowly, typing in between bites.

An hour later he heard a truck door slam at the end of his driveway. He walked to the front window and saw Vance coming towards the porch. He opened the door and stepped outside.

"I guess you've heard by now?"

"Dude," Vance said loudly as he climbed the steps, "you will live in infamy with the park service. Everyone over there is cursing your name. They think you're bad news. Hell, Quincey even threatened to drive over here and shoot you himself but then he saw skunk tracks in the gravel next to his car. He thought it was some evil omen. I just drove over here because I have one question for you."

"And what is that?"

"Did you bait the skunks?"

"I don't know anything about animals Vance, I'm not certified," Catawba said with a smirk.

"That's what I thought you would say."

"So how is Quincey making out?"

"That was hilarious. Lenny made him climb out of the water and sit down in the back of the dumptruck. He drove him up to the maintenance shed and told him to get out and wash himself off with the water hose but instead he took off for his car. He shrieked when he saw skunk tracks in the dirt. Then he just sat down on the ground and started sobbing. When I left Lenny was using industrial cleaning solvents and a pressure washer on him."

"Well it sucks to be him then. I wonder if he'll come after me sometime?"

"If I were you I wouldn't worry too much about it. I've seen stuff like this in the park service before and with that kind of trauma he'll probably just quit and move on."

"Tell Ranger Lansing that I'm sorry but the park service isn't for me."

"Anything you want me to tell Mooseberg?"

"Tell him if he ever wants to go count the ducks on Lake Michigan I will buy the boxes myself and help him pack."

"Damn dude you are one of a kind," Vance said loudly with a laugh.

"I do have a favor to ask you though."

"Sure, what's that?"

"I need you to fill out my final timesheet for me. I didn't do it and I would hate to lose out on that money."

"Don't worry man. I'll see that you get paid. I'll call them myself. I spent six months working in the payroll department at the capital. They even gave me a bronze plaque for it."

"Sure, sure they did Vance."

Vance smiled and nodded and extended his hand. They shook firmly and he turned around and walked down the porch steps and headed for the truck. He climbed inside and back out into the road. He yelled something out the truck window but Catawba couldn't make it out. Then he took off up the road in a flash and disappeared out of sight. Catawba walked over to the porch swing and sat down and started thinking about the day.

21

Two days later he walked in the backdoor of his grandfather's house. The kitchen smelled of burnt meat and the air was as hot as a furnace. He got a piece of paper and a pen from atop the counter and walked around looking in the cabinets. He scribbled down a few things that were needed and then went on to the refrigerator. The inside was bare except for a platter of livermush and a small bowl of cooked cabbage. He winced and shut the door. He wrote down a few more things before tucking the list in the back pocket of his hiking shorts .

"Hey Pop, where are you at?" he asked loudly.

"I'm in here in the living room," the old man responded.

Catawba walked to the living room and found his grandfather tinkering with the rivets on his walker.

"What's wrong with your walker?"

"I was just checking these little metal things. I wanted to see if everything was working good. The nurse messed with it when she came by the other day. She could have broken something on it."

"I'm not quite sure that's possible but okay. Say, did that guy fix your clock or windmill yet?

"No, he said he needs some parts or something. I think he's a crook."

"And why do you say that?"

"The way he eyes my stuff and studies on things."

"Well he's your project not mine. I'm going to the grocery store for you today. I made a list of your necessaries."

"When are you going?"

"Right now, here in a minute."

"Okay, thank you. How's your job at the park service going?"

"Pop, they dismissed me. They said I wasn't a good fit for the organization."

"And what are you going to do now? You've had about every job this part of the country has to offer and you've quit or been fired from all of them."

"I don't know, but sometimes it's better to do nothing than something you hate."

"How's the class at school going then?"

"It's what I expected. I just sit there and go through the motions like most everything in life. We haven't been graded on anything yet and the class is halfway over. I did write an essay and a pretty wild free verse poem for the class though."

"That doesn't sound very honest for the money you paid."

"I know but what can I do?"

Catawba stepped back and watched the old man shake his head and stand up. He clutched the walker and looked up and headed out of the living room. Catawba followed behind him as he went to the bedroom. The old man sat down on the edge of the bed and kicked off his slippers.

"What are you doing Pop?"

"I want to go with you," he replied as he put on his loafers.

The old man grabbed the walker, stood up and took off for the kitchen. He went through the room and headed for the backdoor. Then he went outside and to the car. He opened the rear door and turned around and looked at his grandson.

"Catawba make sure the door is locked."

He pulled the door closed and walked to the car and got in. His grandfather stowed the walker away, shut the rear door, and got in the front seat. Catawba put the car in gear and they circled around and took off down the driveway.

"Is there somewhere special you want to go?" Catawba asked as he cut onto the main highway.

"No, I just wanted to get out of the house."

"Okay, that's fine then."

He drove down the road with his grandfather looking out the window at the passing houses and mailboxes. Occasionally he would point out some building or place that he remembered from his childhood. Catawba listened in silence to the history lesson as he drove down the road.

They pulled into the parking lot of the big box grocery store and Catawba cut the car off and opened his door. His grandfather looked around for a moment and then opened his door too. He wheeled himself around and stood up and got the walker from the backseat. Catawba asked him if he needed some help but he didn't respond. Then they took off walking together across the parking lot. When they went through the sliding glass doors his grandfather stopped abruptly and began studying the motorized carts parked in a row. He pushed the walker against the wall and climbed onto the closest one.

"Do you know how to use one of them?" Catawba asked gently.

"I see the old people on TV using them all the time," he replied as he fingered at the levers.

He pulled back on the right lever and the cart lunged forward causing Catawba to take a step back. He took off into the store with his grandson following behind him. He headed for the produce section and stopped next to a big bin of root vegetables. He stood up and tore off a plastic bag and worked it open with the tips of his fingers. He dug out two big sweet potatoes and put them in the bag and sat back down.

"That's not on the list," Catawba said.

"Yeah but I want some."

He put the bag in the basket of the cart and climbed back on and took off again, bobbing and weaving indifferently through the other customers as he went. He drove over to the meat department and stopped in front of the glass display case and began looking inside like a kid eyeing candy.

"Hey butcher," he called out.

"Yes sir," replied the aproned man behind the counter.

"I want you to cut me a couple of really thick steaks."

The butcher looked at Catawba. He nodded in approval and the butcher went to sawing away at a slab of beef. The old man tapped Catawba in the ribs a time or two and pointed at the meat as the butcher weighed it and wrapped it in wax paper. He slapped a price sticker on it and handed it to Catawba and he dropped it down into the basket and they continued on. The old man drove to the far side of the store and headed down the dairy aisle. He snagged a small brick of unsalted Amish butter and put it in the cart and took off again. Catawba followed along until they reached the registers back at the front of the store. Then he squeezed his grandfather's shoulder.

"I need you to wait here Pop," he whispered in his ear.

"And why's that?"

"Because I have to go get the things we actually came here for. You wait here."

"Okay."

He walked over to the carts and pulled one out and came back. He sat his grandfather's items in his cart and headed for the produce section to start. He worked his way through the store marking things off as he went. When he got back to the front of the store he found his grandfather pestering a young freckle-faced bagboy. He smiled at the kid and touched his grandfather's shoulder.

" You ready to go checkout?"

"Yeah," he responded.

He pushed the cart into an empty checkout lane and began unloading the stuff onto the conveyor belt. The cashier scanned the items quickly and bagged them as she went. Then she totaled up the bill and told him the price.

"Hey I think I left my wallet in my other pair of pants," the old man said slyly.

"I knew you would say something like," Catawba said as he dug his wallet out. "I can read you like a book."

"I hope that book is some grand epic."

"No Pop, if you were a book it would be one about a mischievous child that torments others."

His grandfather laughed as the cashier handed him the change and the receipt. He loaded the bags up in the cart and headed for the exit with grandfather following right behind him. He stopped at the glass double doors to let his grandfather trade out the motorized cart for the walker. Then he pushed the cart out to the car and loaded up the groceries in the trunk while his grandfather put the walker in the backseat and got in. Catawba shut the trunk and pushed the cart into the return and walked back and got behind the wheel.

He drove up the highway slowly, nodding and asking questions as he listened to more stories and events that were unknown to the history books. When he got close to the house he slowed down almost to a crawl and looked over at his grandfather.

"Do you want to stop by the cemetery?"

"Huh?"

"Do you want to go? Yes or no?"

"Shut up and just go on to the house."

Catawba sped up and went to the house. He parked the car around back and got out. He went to the trunk and opened it up and started divvying up the groceries. His grandfather got out, retrieved his walker, and went over to the door and unlocked it. He went inside and headed to the kitchen table and sat down. Catawba came in shortly thereafter carrying an armload of bags. He sat them down on the countertop next to the stove. Then he put everything up except for the plastic bag with the meat and potatoes in it.

"Where's your walker at?"

"I left it next to the backdoor."

"Well, do you want me to cook your feast for you?"

"Yes, if you don't mind. I think respectable people should have a nice meal every now and again ."

"Respectable people huh? I think respectable people probably buy their own groceries and don't try to pull some quick con on their grandchildren."

"Shut up. You know I'm on a fixed income."

"Yeah and I'm on no income."

The old man laughed and Catawba shook his head. He grabbed the grocery sack and sat the items out. He washed the sweet potatoes in the sink and dried them with a handtowel . He brought the potatoes back to the stove and wrapped them in aluminum foil and placed them on a baking sheet. He turned the oven on and put them inside.

"Those will be ready in a little bit," he said as he got out a frying pan.

"Thank you for doing this for me."

"No problem. Don't forget you have a VA appointment this month."

"What for?"

"It's time for your yearly check up. I'll come over early that day and get you."

His grandfather didn't respond as he pushed himself up from the table and went around getting out the crockery and silverware. He set the table and asked Catawba what he wanted to drink. He told him water and the old man took two glasses to the faucet and filled them up. He brought them back to the table and sat them down and fished two napkins out of the holder and put them between the two plates. He sat back down in his chair and stared out the window.

Catawba watched him for a moment, then he turned around and lopped off a big piece of butter and put it in the pan. He turned the heat on and stood there watching as it slowly liquified. He salt and peppered the steaks and placed them in the pan. He washed his hands and went to the table.

"We'll eat the steaks first because those sweet potatoes will take a good hour to cook."

"Okay."

He sat down and looked over at the clock on the wall. The clock was an hour off but still held its minutes true. After a few minutes he got up and walked over to the stove and flipped the steaks. He went to the refrigerator and opened the door and started rummaging through the condiments.

"What are you looking for?"

"Steak sauce. I remember you used to keep it in here."

"This isn't a steakhouse so you'll just have to make do."

"Okay."

He returned to the stove and cut the eye off and turned around to his grandfather. He listened for a moment to the steady ticking cadence of the wall clock and then spoke.

"She fixed this for you didn't she?"

"Yes she did. Steak and sweet potatoes was one of my favorite meals and she fixed it quite often."

"Well why didn't you want to go by the cemetery today? You could have seen her grave?"

"Catawba, a grave is just a patch of neglected dirt and a hunk of rock with some words written on it. To really remember someone you have to use your senses. If you were old you would understand that and if you understood that you would understand why I don't leave this house."

"I'm sorry. I shouldn't have said anything about it."

"Well don't be," the old man said as he pushed himself up from the table.

Catawba watched his grandfather leave the kitchen and head for the living room. He went over and sat down at the head of the table and waited and listened but his grandfather didn't come back and he didn't call out.

When the potatoes got done baking he got them out of the oven and sat the pan on top of the stove. He let them cool off and then forked them into a big plastic bowl and put the meat on top. He took it to the refrigerator and put it inside and headed for the living room.

His grandfather was sitting on the couch with a pillow in his lap. He sat down in a chair across from him and waited for him to speak but he didn't. A few minutes went by and he heard a gentle slamming coming from outside. He got up and looked out the window and saw the mailman pulling away from the mailbox. He opened the door and went out. He walked down through the yard and got the mail out of the box. He walked back up to the house slowly, looking at the junk mail as he went. He opened the door and went to the trashcan and threw it all away. He walked back and leaned against the paint chipped door frame. His grandfather was lying on his back staring up at the ceiling. He sighed and walked back through the house and went out the backdoor. He got in his car and sped home.

He pulled into the driveway and got out and shut the door. He looked over at his neighbor's place, both of them were comatose in beach chairs and sunburnt. He sighed and went around to the back of the house and disappeared through the door. He clicked his tongue a couple of times and the cat came trotting out from under a kitchen chair. He reached down, scooped him up, and sat him on his shoulders. Then he went over to the counter, picked up the bag of food, and headed for the car.

He opened the door and sat the food in the passenger's seat. He lifted the cat off his shoulders and sat him in between the seats and then got in too. He closed the door and let out another long sigh. He put the car in gear and headed back to his grandfather's house.

He pulled up behind the house and got out with the bag in one hand and the cat in the other. He went through the backdoor and sat the cat down on the kitchen floor. He walked to the door of the living room and popped his head into the room.

"Hey Pop."

"What? What do you want?" the old man asked without moving.

"I put the food in the refrigerator. It's in tupperware and you can eat it whenever."

He waited for the old man to respond but he didn't. He turned around, went back to the kitchen, and got out two bowls. He filled one with water and the other one with kibble and sat them down next to the credenza. He walked back into the living room and stood over the couch. His grandfather stared up at him but didn't say anything.

"I got something to keep you company. You'll have to let him outside to use the bathroom but don't worry, he's too old to run away. I put some food and water down for him."

"What? What are you talking about?"

"You'll see. He'll come in here when he gets through exploring the house."

Catawba took off back to the kitchen and scooped the cat up off the countertop and carried him to the entrance of the living room. He sat him down, closed his eyes tightly, and exhaled. Then he turned around and dashed out of the house and left.

22

Wednesday morning he walked into the classroom to find a young man standing behind the lectern. The man was looking around in mild consternation and nervously clicking an ink pen. Catawba sat down in his normal seat and took his paper out of his rucksack. He glanced at it for a moment before looking up. Then he felt a tap on his arm and heard a voice.

"I want you to apologize for what you said."

He turned to his left and saw Neveva staring at him. He racked his brain for a minute but he quickly gave up.

"What did I say? I just walked into the classroom and sat down."

"About the city. Apologize for saying that about Fonta Flora."

"I'm not sure what you're talking about. Is this a cultural thing?"

"No, this is not some cultural thing," she responded.

"Ok then, have it your way. Nevena I am sincerely sorry for whatever it is I did or said. In the future I will try my best to refrain from such conduct. Feel better now?"

"Were you being sincere?"

"Of course I was. I even used that very word."

"We'll see," she replied.

"Okay class everyone look at me," the young man at the front said loudly. "My name is Dr. Kellen and I'm going to fill in today since Binetti is not here."

"Well where is he?" someone asked.

"He called in sick today."

"Well what's wrong with him? He's so inspirational."

"He has a hangover but please don't tell anyone I told you. That could get me in trouble."

121

"Don't worry sir, my lips are sealed."

"That's good. Now guys I am the head of the Science department but I am more than qualified to fill in for a humanities class. I'm going to grade your homework while you watch a video on something I choose. Make sure your names are on your papers and bring them up here."

Dr. Kellen walked to the corner and pulled the wheeled TV stand to the front of the room. Catawba picked up his paper and stood up. He grabbed Nevena's paper and carried both of them to the lectern and sat them on top of the other two. Then he turned around and walked back and sat down.

"Give me a second here," he called out as he rifled through the dusty DVD tapes.

Nevena looked over at Catawba and rolled her eyes. He smiled as he tapped his fingers on top of the desk.

"The humidity is miserable here in this country," she whispered. "It's hot where I come from but not like this."

"Hey, I just remembered something."

"And what did you just remember?"

"I just remembered that you never told me what country you're from or what you do for a living."

"I'm from…"

Their heads and eyes shot forward as the TV flashed to life. On the screen appeared a young woman in period costume. She was walking alongside the River Thames and speaking with an Oxford accent. Dr. Kellen walked over and cut off the lights. He came back and gathered up the papers and sat down at the desk and started making marks with his pen.

When the class was half over Catawba looked over at Nevena. Her head was tilted back and she was slightly slobbering. He tapped her shoulder a few times and she came to life.

"Damn it Catawba, what's wrong?"

"You're missing the best part. They're about to go on a guided tour of Winchester Cathedral."

She said something in her native tongue and put her head back down on the desk. He sighed and looked around the room. The other students were as still as statues but

Kellen was staring at him and frantically tapping his pen. Before he could speak Kellen got up and darted out of the classroom with the papers in hand. Catawba shrugged it off and continued watching the video.

Kellen came back into the classroom as the credits started to roll. He cut the lights on and walked up to the lectern.

"Read the next chapter in the textbook," he said loudly.

Nevena zipped her bag closed and rubbed her eyes. She got up slowly and then followed the other two out. Catawba stood up and shouldered his rucksack as he studied the piercing eyes of Kellen.

"Mr. Fox, I need you to follow me up to the administration building," Kellen said sternly.

Catawba didn't respond as he walked to the door and started following behind Dr. Kellen. They walked to the side entrance of the building and went outside. They walked up a long set of cement steps toward the administration building. Then they entered a set of double glass doors and walked over to a long row of chairs.

"Please sit down right here Mr. Fox," Kellen said with a small hand gesture.

"What did I do?"

"You need some serious professional help," he replied as he walked away.

Catawba sat down and looked around. The walls were decorated with next to nil and the various college functionaries typed away at their desktops with lethargic intensity. Then his eyes settled on a big window that looked out over the campus and toward the former hayfield. The ryegrass was gone and the grading equipment was parked in a row. A massive slab of concrete rested atop the red dirt square and yellow vested men scurried back and forth. It just never ends around here, he thought. After a few minutes a door to his left popped open and the dean stuck his head outside and looked at him.

"Catawba Fox," the dean whispered.

"Yes?"

"Come in here for a minute," he replied as he opened the door, "We need to have a discussion."

Catawba stood up and walked into the office. The dean told him to close the door and he did so without protest. He sat down in a chair and looked across the desk. The dean glanced down at the paper and rubbed his forehead. Then he leaned back in the chair, put his hands on his stomach, and looked at him.

"Mr. Fox, I'm one of the deans here at the junior college. Do you remember talking to me a few weeks ago?"

"Vaguely."

"Do you know how long I've been here in this room?"

"I don't know sir. I guess since you got here this morning."

"Yes, yes, of course since this morning but do you know how long I've had this job?"

"I don't know but I have a feeling you're going to tell me."

"Twenty-five years. I moved to this area twenty-five years ago to take this job and in twenty-five years I have learned one immutable truth. Do you know what that is?"

"I have no idea."

"The immutable truth is that you people are your own worst enemies. You see Mr. Fox this area is peppered with people just like you. People who believe they can gum up the works of progress if they cause enough havoc. And that," he said as he leaned forward and rested his arms on the desk, "is exactly what this paper is. Isn't it?"

"That paper is an assignment on current events and how nobody listens to anyone anymore and what happens if we don't start...."

"That's very amusing Mr. Fox. It's so amusing I'm not even going to let you finish your thought. Do you have dreams?"

"Doesn't everyone sir?"

"Of course everyone has dreams. That's just part of the human experience. Do you know what my dream has been for the last twenty-four and half years?"

"I have no idea sir. What's your dream?"

"I've always dreamed about getting the opportunity to pick up the phone right here on this desk and call down to the state psychiatric hospital and have one of you damn Fonta Florans put in a padded cell. How's that for a dream?"

"To each his own I guess. What does that have to do with me?"

"Because with this," he said as he tapped his fingers on top of the paper, "I have the very thing I need to make my dream come true. How does that make you feel?"

"Do you want me to tell you the truth?"

"Of course I do."

"I don't have any feelings whatsoever when it comes to you or people like you or places like this. How's that?"

"You don't understand young man . In my hands I hold the power to have you sent to the…"

"You're the lunatic," Catawba said loudly as he stood up. "You don't have any power whatsoever. You're just another blowhard sitting behind a desk trying to get attention, and this area is not peppered with people like me, it's peppered with people like you. People who roll into town, buy a house, and then finagle their way into some pointless desk job. But I'm going to let you in on a little secret."

"And what's that?"

"I'm about to walk outside into the fresh air and sunshine. You, on the other hand, are going to be left sitting alone here in this office. But don't worry, you'll still sit there believing that the world revolves around you, but it doesn't, and it never did."

Catawba turned around and hurried out of the office without waiting for a response. He went over to the glass doors and disappeared outside. He walked down to the parking lot and got in his car and left for home.

He pulled into his driveway and got out. He leaned up against the side of the car and watched as a multitude of Chimney swifts flew in quick circles above the roof of the house. After a few minutes he smiled, grabbed his rucksack, and went inside. He closed all the curtains and checked the phone. He put some sardines and a sleeve of crackers in his pack and filled up a gallon jug with water. He went out the backdoor and down to the basement. He got out the canoe and tossed his stuff inside and drug it over to the driveway. He stopped in the gravel and looked over at his neighbor's place.

125

Everything was silent and the only movement was the flapping of the flags in the wind.

He readjusted his grip and began dragging the canoe down the driveway. He stopped at the road to let a car pass and then continued on down the hill until he came to the big rocks of the shore. He walked to the rear of the canoe and gave it a big shove into the lake. He walked back and eased himself down through the rocks until he was standing in the water. Then he grabbed the nose of the canoe and yanked it beside him. He climbed inside and picked up the paddle and set off.

He paddled with celerity out of the cove and into the main channel of the lake as the sun baked down on the firmament in the high humidity of June. He paddled for a good hour until he was in sight of the largest island on the lake. He sat the paddle aside and studied it for any sign of life or occupancy but decided it was empty. Then he retook the paddle and picked up the pace.

He beached the canoe on the southside of the island and climbed out. He pulled the canoe up a small slope and hid it behind a massive white pine. He took a big swig of water and collapsed onto the dirt and pine needles and didn't move for some time.

When he stirred again the sun was starting to set over the blue hued mountains to the west. He stood up and tried to wipe the sweat and grime off his body but ended up with a smeared mess. He grabbed the jug of water and uncapped it and raised it to his lips and had a long drink as he looked out across the water. The clouds to the east were outlined in orange but didn't move. Then he recapped the jug and sat it down beside the canoe. He stood there listening for any sign of approaching boats but he heard nothing of concern. He got the lighter out of his pack and pocketed it and took off in a cautious walk towards the center of the island.

He found a couple of granite rocks at the base of a small poplar tree and sat about arranging them in a circle. He took his hand and leveled out the ground before setting each stone. He stood up and looked at his primitive fire pit and smiled. He kicked the ground with the toe of his shoe and began walking around picking up pinecones and kindling sticks.

When he finished collecting the combustibles he walked back and sat everything on the ground. He knelt down and mounded up the pinecones and propped the kindling sticks up into a teepee. He dug the lighter out of his pocket and struck it at the base of the wood. After a few seconds the pine resin popped and cracked and then caught. He stood up and watched as the flames slowly engulfed the wood illuminating the ground and trees in front of him.

He turned around and made a slow retreat back to his water and rucksack, flicking the lighter every couple of steps to check for roots and holes. When he got to the canoe he looked out across the lake. The big mansions on the distant shore were dark and tombic and nothing moved inside of them. He stood there for a while watching the white-capping of the small waves as they washed up onto the sandy shore. Then he sighed and reached down and grabbed his water and his pack. He turned round and headed back as the nocturnal serenading of the katydids reached its fever pitch.

When he got back to the fire he sat his stuff down on the ground and tossed a few sticks of wood into the flames. He eased himself down onto the cool earth and got out his food. He nibbled on the crackers and chased them with the juice from the sardine cans. He wiped his mouth with the back of his grimy hand and sipped the tepid water from the jug. He ate the little oily filets of fish one by one as the fire undulated with the breeze. He popped the lid back on top of the water and sat the empty tins next to him. Then he folded his legs up against his chest, put his head between his knees, and sat there breathing heavily as the moon rose in the east.

He was awakened at dawn by the trilling of a screech owl on the far side of the island. He sat up and looked at the spent fire. The ashes were milky white and cold. He took a deep breath and looked around for his water and rucksack but they were gone. He leapt to his feet and began looking at the ground for any signs of footprints. There was nothing noticeable other than the ones he had made the night before. The owl trilled again and he took off running for the canoe.

When he got there he discovered that his canoe had vanished. He looked out across the lake and saw a few fishermen near the rocks on the far shore. He picked up a piece of driftwood and slammed it against a tree. Then he turned around and started walking back across the island, finding nothing as he went except for a few small cairns and litter from previous pilgrims.

As he got close to the other side of the island he heard a man's voice. He took off running through the thick underbrush and came out onto a small sandbar. He saw a frail man in a small fishing boat. He was forty yards offshore and singing as if he were trying to lure the fish by melody. Catawba called out to the man and he stopped singing. He reeled in his line and sat his pole down inside the boat. Then he walked to the trolling motor and started guiding the boat toward the sandbar.

"Good morning," Catawba said as the boat drew near.

"It'd be better if you hadn't disturbed my fishing," the old fellow replied. "What do you want?"

"I camped out here on the island last night and when I woke up this morning all my stuff was gone."

"What'd you expect? People in these parts will steal anything not nailed down."

"Well I hope they're happy. I loved that rucksack and canoe."

"This world is full of mischief young feller. Do you want me to carry you across the lake to where you live?"

"That would be the greatest charity I have ever received."

"Which shore do you live on?"

"I live on Laurel Lane close to the park."

"I'm not taking you there but I'll take you to the shore in front of this island. That'd be just too far for me to go in my tiny boat."

"That would be perfect. I can walk home from there."

"Climb in then."

Catawba wadded out to the aluminum boat and grabbed the stern cleat. He pulled himself up and over the gunwale and rolled over onto his back and looked up at the man.

"You sure do look a   sight young man. You look like an escapee from a traveling freak show. You need to take a bath and get the grime off of your face."

"I couldn't agree with you more. My name is Catawba."

"My name's Moses but I'm not a prophet. It's just my name."

"Nice to meet you Moses. What do you do?"

"Do? Don't you see all this white hair on my head? I'm almost eighty-five years old. I fish for food these days but thirty years ago I worked at a mill but then they went and closed it down. What do you do?"

"I'm a writer or at least that's what I tell people. But I'm not well traveled and I don't have much luck in society."

"That's a tough one there. I remember years ago when they gave me my notice at the mill. They said they would pay for me to go back to school. Said I could learn to type and work in an office. I told them at my age I would rather spend my days fishing than working. Jobs can go on forever but a man's life can't.

"You're alright Moses."

"I make it day by day like we all do," he replied as he cranked the outboard motor.

Catawba nodded and Moses pushed the throttle forward. The motor groaned and then took off.

As they drew close to the shore Catawba stepped to the nose of the boat and jumped off onto the sandy beach. He turned around and looked back at the man.

"Don't worry young man," he yelled out as he backed the boat up. "You keep going and you may find the promised land yet."

Catawba turned around and headed across the sand for the embankment. He stopped when he got there and looked up at the steep slope to see that It was choked with blooming kudzu and sawbriars. Then he clenched his teeth and started climbing.

He stopped when he was halfway up and tried to dislodge the thorns that had bitten into his arms and legs but most of them just broke off under the skin. He heard a car passing above him and he took off climbing again. He stepped up on the top of a large root and found himself staring at the aluminum guardrail of the dam road. He grabbed the hot metal post and pulled himself up and onto the shoulder of the road. He stepped over the guardrail and took off walking.

The kudzu gulleys next to the spillway bridge teemed with the buzzing of insects and the cicadas sang out from their secret stations. Logging trucks loaded down with heavy timber shot by him, stirring up the humid air, and littering the road with big shards of bark. He stopped near the end of the bridge and looked towards the east. A smoke rose up near the edge of the city but he couldn't make out its source. After a few seconds he turned back toward the road and continued on.

He stopped when he got to the earthen dam and took his wet shoes off. He stripped off his filthy socks and put them in his pocket. He tested the temperature of the asphalt with the tip of his big toe and nodded. He put his wet shoes under his armpits and took off in a brisk trot using the littered tree bark as stepping stones along the way.

He slowed down when he reached the other side of the dam and stepped off the road and onto the grassy shoulder and knelt down and wiped the little flakes of wood off his bare feet. He stood up to see a sheriff's department patrol car creeping his way with its overhead lights on. He stood stockstill watching as the cruiser stopped and a portly deputy got out.

"Where are you coming from," the deputy asked loudly, "and why are you covered with scratches and mud?"

"I camped out on the big island last."

"I see and how did you get out there? Swim?"

"I took my canoe but someone swiped it from me in the middle of the night. A man named Moses carried me back to the shore."

"Moses huh? Get your ass over here boy," the deputy said as he waved his hand.

Catawba walked to the side of the car where the deputy stood. The deputy slapped the front fender and he sat his shoes down on the ground and placed his hands on top of the

130

hot metal. The deputy stepped behind him and kicked his legs apart.

"What's your name son?"

"Catawba Fox."

"That's rich," the deputy said as he patted him down. "Do you have any ID on you?"

"No sir, I never take anything like that when I'm out in nature."

"And why's that?"

"Because I know who I am."

"Well did you know that it's a crime to impede traffic around here?"

"I give up man," he replied.

The deputy twisted his arms behind his back and cuffed him. Then he grabbed his shoulder and led him to the back of the car. He opened the rear door and shoved him inside. He slammed the door and went to the front of the car and dug out his cellphone. Catawba put his head against the window and tried to listen to the conversation but he couldn't make anything out. After a few minutes the deputy opened the driver's side door and got in.

"Where do you live son?"

"I live right up the road here on Laurel Lane."

"I'm going to take your ass home and don't you do this again."

"Thank you sir."

The deputy started the car and took off. Catawba told him which house and the deputy drove there quickly. He pulled into the driveway and hopped out and opened the backdoor and yanked him outside and onto the ground. Then he undid the manacles and waved at him to go. Catawba got up and turned around and walked away without speaking. He walked up onto the porch, opened the front door, and disappeared inside. He went to the kitchen sink and chugged two cups of water. Then he stripped off his clothes and tossed them in the washing machine and went to the bathroom and took a long shower.

After he dried off he doused the cuts on his legs with peroxide and put on fresh clothes. He went searching around for his shoes but then he shouted and kicked the wall. He walked outside and got in his car and drove over to where the deputy picked him up. He cussed under his breath as he walked over to the ditch and picked up his shoes.

23

The next day he drove over to his grandfather's house. When he walked through the backdoor he felt a pleasant rush of cool air. He went through the house and headed for the living room . The old man was sitting on the couch with the cat in his lap.

"Well I see you guys are getting along great."

"Yeah I had to turn the air conditioning on for him."

"You could've turned it on anytime. You don't need a special guest to be comfortable."

"Catawba I am not going to get into it with you over the utilities again."

He sat down in the chair and heard something different. He looked around the room and saw the cuckoo clock ticking away on the wall.

"I see that guy fixed the clock for you."

"Yes he did. He said he figured out how to fix it from a library book and here I sat believing you were an expert in books."

"Just as long as it gets fixed. How's the cat doing?"

"Tomcat is doing good ."

"You named him Tomcat? Wow, that's very original."

"You never told me his name so I gave him one and Tomcat is the only name I could think of for a cat. I don't think I am going to give him back either. I like him too much."

Catawba sighed and looked out the window. He stood up and went around the house looking at the medicines and food. He made a small list of things but decided to throw it away. He checked the bedsheets and emptied the little trash cans. Then he walked back to the living room and sat back down.

"Are you making it to the mailbox alright? The doctor said walking is good for your hip ."

"Ah," the old man said as he rubbed the cat, "I usually call that kid who mows my grass and he gets it for me."

"You have to walk on your hip Pop. The doctor said so and more than just inside the house. Otherwise you'll end up in a wheelchair and you don't want that because you'll end up in a rest home."

"It will be alright just trust me."

"I'm not going to argue with you anymore."

"It wouldn't do any good anyway. How've you been lately?"

"Well let's see, in the past two days I've run away from school, had my canoe and rucksack stolen, and got arrested. I really hated losing that rucksack too. I bought it years ago when I went hiking up on the Appalachian Trail. I even took the time to sew my initials on top."

"I knew it was only a matter of time with the school. I don't know why I even suggested it," the old man said calmly. "You're too bullheaded for instruction. Wait, what did you get arrested for?"

"I got escorted home I guess you could say. I was walking along the road that goes over the dams and the cop said I was in the way of traffic."

"Did you tell the cop that someone stole your stuff?"

"To tell you the truth I don't think that cop would have cared."

"What are you going to do now about a job? I think we both know your name is not very high up on the list of people to hire around here."

"I'm supposed to help the neighbors build their log cabin next week. Can I ask you an honest question?"

"I guess so."

"What would you think about us selling our homes and moving away? You always said you wanted to go out west again."

"Catawba Fox," the old man snapped, "I'm not selling this house ever. I will die in this house and you know why. I never want you to ask me that question again. If you want to leave here go ahead but I'm staying put."

He went to say something else but stopped. He got up and walked out onto the front porch and sat down in the faded porch swing. The road in front of the house was peaceful and the June bugs buzzed about the yard in lazy patterns. As time marched on he heard the front door shut and his grandfather took a seat in the rocking chair next to him.

"The grass needs rain," he said with a wave of his hand. "I don't even mow mine anymore. What would be the point? There's no one to even look at it. It seems that everyone in our clan has gone on to the cemetery or moved away. I'm not quite sure about this place anymore. Maybe we're not really tied to a place. Maybe we're just tied to the people who lived there and the memories of our youth."

"Catawba, if you want to go away don't let me stop you. I'll have someone else get my groceries if need be."

"Just let me think about it for a while and let's see what they say at your VA appointment. Besides, I don't have the money to move away right now."

"Listen to me, just because people die doesn't mean you have to die with them."

He froze and stopped swinging. He folded his arms up against his stomach and looked over at the old man. He was rocking slowly and his head was beaded with sweat. He looked back at the yard as the slight whispers of air stirred up the summer heat.

The next morning he was walking around the farmers market with several pokes of produce and a hankering for goat cheese. He walked past the musician and headed for the chevre booth.

"How's life been treating you Catawba? How's the lake? You've missed a couple of weeks," the farmer said when he walked up.

"I've been making the rounds. Say, I've never thought of asking you your name."

"My name is Ben. I've told you that about a dozen times but you're always hungry. It just goes in one ear and right out the other."

"Oh."

"Don't worry it's okay. Where've you been?"

"I worked a few weeks for the park service but they had to let me go. Say, do you happen to have any of those big logs of cheese?"

"I have one with honey and ground walnuts. It weighs nearly two pounds."

"That'll do. I want one of those and a plastic spoon too."

"Give me a second."

He turned around to the cooler and got out a large wax papered log of cheese. He sat it on the side of the booth table and handed over a small plastic spoon. Catawba handed him the money, unwrapped the log, and started chiseling off small globs of goat cheese and eating them.

"You know man," he said lazily between bites, "I believe this is the only thing in this city worth having."

"I really like it too. I tried cows but they're just too big. I think I might be the only one here who makes goat cheese but I don't know. It started off as just a hobby but when they closed the plant down I began doing it full time. It pays the bills so I can't complain."

"Maybe I should go into goat farming with you. I need to find something to do for money."

"Son, I want you to look down," he said shrewdly. "You have inhaled four dollars worth of goat cheese in the time we've been talking. You would lose your ass in farming."

Catawba looked down at the log and grunted. He tossed the spoon over into the wastebasket and began rewrapping the cheese but stopped when he felt a vibration coming from atop his hiking shoe. He looked down to see a Pomeranian bouncing up and down on its forepaws. He looked up again and found himself face to face with an olive skinned man holding a leash.

"Catawba Fox," the man cried out, "I haven't seen you since the county kulning contest up at the lake. How've you been?"

"I'm always the same. I stick to myself and don't bother anyone."

"That's interesting," the man said quickly, "since that day a few years back I have completely revolutionized my life. I am no longer concerned with the ephemeral. I eschew everything

135

transitory and study instead upon the fundamental elements of the cosmos. I even took a month long sabbatical to India where I studied under the grand yogi…"

Catawba stood there listening to the man's frantic oration on the mysteries of life. He tried to keep up but he soon found himself siding with the little dog who was now firmly pulling the leash in the other direction. After a few minutes the man stopped talking, tipped his trilby, and dashed off through the market with his dog in tow. Catawba looked over at Ben. He was sitting on the tailgate of his truck and smiling.

"You sure do know some strange characters."

"But why is it always me?"

"What? What do you mean?"

"Nothing I guess. I think I'll go home now. See you next week."

He picked up the cheese log and slid it down into one of the paper pokes. He walked back to the center of the market and stopped to watch the musician play a folkish mandolin number. Then he went up the hill, loaded up in his car, and left.

He put his groceries up when he got home. Then he kicked off his shoes and laid down for a nap. He was almost out for the count when he heard a loud knocking coming from the front door. Boom. Boom. Boom.

"Damn it I'm coming," he yelled out.

He got up and walked to the front door. He opened it to see Janice standing there in a floral dress three decades past its prime. He walked out onto his porch and looked at her.

"What? What do you want?"

"He's coming. We found him," she replied happily.

"I didn't know anyone was lost but I'm glad he's safe and sound."

"Oh stop it," she said with a light slap on the shoulder. "You Fonta Florans have such a dry sense of humor. Remember I said we were going to hire someone to help us put together our log home?"

"Vaguely."

136

"Don found a master craftsman in the classifieds of the local newspaper. He's even going to give us a senior discount."

" Well wonders never cease."

He walked to the edge of the porch and leaned up against the column. He looked over at his neighbors place and back at Janice.

"Will you do me a favor?"

"Sure Catawba."

"I want you to walk over here to where I am standing and take a good hard look at your property and tell me what you see."

She walked over to where he was standing and stopped. She waved to Don and smiled. Then she turned around and looked at him.

"I see Don smoking a pipe. I see our majestic flags and RV. I see our antique Mercedes. I see my beautiful flowers. I see the log cabin kit that will be our new home. I see the golden years of our retirement being spent in happiness and harmony."

"Oh I see all that too," he replied calmly, "but what I don't see is a foundation on which to set that log home. Are you guys going to have a dirt floor in your house?"

She gave him a hateful look and went stomping off the porch. She walked across the driveway to Don and started yelling. He got up from his lawn chair and went inside the RV. He emerged a few seconds later carrying a magazine. He flipped it open and did some perfunctory pointing at a random page. She wiped the sweat from her forehead, hugged him, and walked back over Catawba.

"Don told me a foundation can always be added after something is built. He is just so smart. Do you still want to help us?"

"I wouldn't miss it for the world. And when do you foresee this master craftsman coming?"

"He'll be here Tuesday morning. He says he likes to beat the heat."

"Janice, I will mark that date down on my calendar. I do enjoy having such extraordinary people in my life."

137

He walked back to the front door and disappeared inside. He latched the door and walked back to the middle of the house and looked out the window. Don was belly down on the clumpy soil and peering at a long level. Janice walked up to him and laid down on the ground too. Catawba laughed as he went back to finish his nap.

24

He was up at sunrise on Tuesday. He used the bathroom and went to look out the window at the neighbor's RV as the coffee perked. There were no sounds and nobody stirred. He went back to the kitchen and quickly drank a cup of coffee. He went to his bedroom and put on his shoes. Then he sighed as he stood up and headed for the door.

The air was already hot and humid as he walked across the driveway and headed for the RV. He inched up to the aluminum door and listened. He heard the soft droning of a small fan but nothing else. He waited a few seconds and started knocking. He heard someone clear their throat and then the door shot open. Don popped his head out and looked at him.

"What do you want?"

"I am supposed to help you guys today with your cabin right?"

"Oh yeah about that," Don said as he stepped out and pulled the door to. "I don't have any money to pay you."

"I was just sort of doing this as a neighborly thing."

"That's the nicest thing anyone has ever done for us. I tell you what, you go back to your house and wait until he gets here. No sense in you standing out here in the heat."

Catawba sighed and took off walking back to his house. He was climbing the back steps when he noticed that Don was tailing him. He stopped and turned around and waited.

"Hey listen man," Don said nervously, "do you happen to have any pot? I'm all out and I cannot stand to be like this. I get the jitters and Janice gets irate. See, she needs to be medicated too."

"I'm sorry but I do good to buy my groceries and pay my bills."

"Well, do you know where to get any? I can pay you when I get my retirement check next month."

"Look," Catawba said as he stepped down onto the ground, "I will help you guys out with your cabin but that's it. I don't want anything to do with drugs or drama."

Don turned around and slinked away quietly. He stood there for a moment and then went inside his house and watered his cactus. He carried it out onto the front porch and sat it down on the railing in the sunlight. Then he eased himself down beside one of the porch columns and listened to a cardinal call out from atop a pawpaw tree near the woodline.

The next day he was typing away at his desk when he heard a door slam. He got up and went over to the window and looked out. A shirtless man with rough features was standing beside a beat up truck talking to Don. Janice came out of the RV and gave them a casual nod as she passed by. She headed on towards the property line in a brisk trot. Catawba walked out onto the front porch and met her.

"I want to apologize for the way Don acted yesterday. He's better now. In fact we both are. Do you still want to help?"

"I'll be right there."

He shut the door and took off behind her. She walked quickly and never looked back. They got to the man's truck as he was donning his toolbelt.

"This is my neighbor Catawba," Don proclaimed loudly. "He's a great guy."

The worker nodded at him as he fumbled with his toolbelt. Catawba told him good morning and then he turned around and looked at Don. His eyes were red and a small patch of spittle painted his chin. Catawba shook his head and walked over to the man.

"I'm not quite sure what to do here. I've never put together a cabin before."

"It'll be alright. I'll teach ya how to do it."

The man cinched his toolbelt tight and walked over to the wood beams and began rummaging around. He motioned at Catawba to get on the other side of the beams and he did. The worker would tap on a log and Catawba would grab the end. They lifted in unison, setting them aside one by one. They did that for an hour until the logs were sorted by size and notch type. Then the man walked over and sat down on the tailgate of his truck with a bewildered look on his face.

"Say," the man said loudly as he uncapped a bottle of water, "whatcha you guys going to do about a foundation for this cabin here?"

"We're going to add it after it's built," Don replied.

"Doesn't work like that."

Catawba and the man watched as Janice got up and went inside the RV. She slammed the door with such force that a floral flag fell from the aluminum roof and landed at Don's feet. He stood there for a moment before going inside the RV too.

"Where did they find you at ?" Catawba asked.

"That Don guy got my number off the back of the newspaper. I told him I was a stonemason and nothing else but he didn't care. Said he'd pay me either way."

"Well, do you know how to put these things together?"

"Son," the man replied as he turned and looked at him, "I've been building stuff for going on forty years and I can tell you this cabin will lay here and rot before it gets completed."

"Then why did you agree to do this for them?"

"I like to watch these people when they don't get their way."

The door of the RV shot open and Janice marched outside carrying a valise. She went to Mercedes and got in. Don walked out slowly and headed for the car too but she put it in gear and drove off before he could reach her. He stood there for a moment looking at the road. Then he walked over and sat down in the lawn chair.

"Just go ahead and put the damn thing together. I'll live in it either way."

"Well where do you want us to put it? The cabin?"

"Just set it up with the front door facing the road," Don said.

"Suit yourself," the man replied.

He motioned at Catawba as he got up. They went over and grabbed the biggest log. They set it in place, bolted it down, and grabbed the next one. They worked steadily for three hours until the four walls were waist high.

"It's hot. Let's take a break," the man said as he tightened down the last bolt.

Catawba wiped the sweat from his forehead and walked over to where Don was sitting. He looked at Don and Don looked back at him.

"What?"

"Do you have anything to drink? It's almost ninety-five degrees out here."

"Oh," he said as he got up, "let me go find you something."

Catawba walked over and sat down on the tailgate of the truck with the man. They sat there together listening to the shuffling of feet and the slamming of cabinet doors coming from inside the RV.

"I don't think he has the money to pay," he said quietly.

"He will when he gets his retirement check or I'll take him to small claims court."

After a few minutes the RV door opened and Don walked out carrying a steaming coffee cup. Catawba smiled as he ambled up to him balancing the cup.

"Here you go, neighbor. I made you some chamomile tea in the microwave. Be careful it's super hot."

"Thank you. I am sure it will be great on this sweltering summer day."

"You bet it will. Janice drinks that stuff all the time. She says it helps her bowels and digestion."

He took the cup and held it out in front of him. Don walked over to the walls and started inspecting the notches and the bolts. Catawba watched him for a moment and then flung the scalding liquids into the weeds. The man grinned as he eased himself up from the tailgate and walked over to Don.

"Everything good?"

"I have this crazy idea," Don replied. "I think we can make the walls bigger but you guys have to take it apart."

"How can you make a square frame bigger? The cabin is prefabricated."

141

"I read a magazine article that said you could. Here let me go get it out of the camper," he said as he walked off.

He went inside the RV and came back out carrying a rolled up magazine. He walked over to the worker and showed him a picture.

"If you say so."

The worker motioned at Catawba to get up. He sat the cup down on the tailgate and walked over to them.

"We're going to take the cabin apart. Don says we can make it bigger if we build it twice."

"I'm not sure it works like that," Catawba said.

"Yeah it does," the worker said with a wink. "Don has it all figured out."

"Okay then."

They started taking the cabin apart as Don went back to his chair. They undid the fastener bolts and unstacked the logs in no time. Then they restacked the logs into piles and looked over at Don.

"We're going to start putting it back together again," the worker said loudly.

"Make it bigger. Try to widen the frame," Don replied.

"Are you still going to pay me when you get your retirement check?'

"You know it."

The worker looked at Catawba and nodded and they started reassembling the cabin walls. The work went quicker this time as they reset the logs exactly the same. They stopped again when the walls were waist high and looked over at Don who was napping in the chair.

"Hey Don," the worker called out loudly.

He opened his eyes and got up and walked over to them and looked around. He stepped back and scratched his chin.

"Why is it not bigger?"

"Sir," the worker said slowly, "we tried every trick in the book but we couldn't find a way to make the frame bigger. It's almost like the cabin is supposed to be the size you ordered."

"Why," Don said in a flash of anger, "I think you're trying to hoodoo me. I think you did something to it while I was asleep. I've got something for your ass. You just wait right here."

He marched over to the RV and disappeared inside. The worker took off his toolbelt and slung it in the back of the truck. Then he walked over to the driver's side door as Catawba stood there watching everything. In no time Don came charging back out of the RV with an ancient cricket bat. The worker gave him the finger and got in the truck and pulled away just as Don swung the bat. The bat missed and the momentum made him face plant into the red clay dirt. Catawba walked over and helped him up.

"Are you alright?"

"Yeah," he said as he tried to wipe the dirt off. "I pegged him for a con artist the minute he pulled up. I just didn't say anything though, it was Janice's adventure. Say, do you know anything about landscaping?"

"I guess it is self explanatory."

"That's a good attitude to have. Now I want you to go home and come back in the morning. It's too hot now."

"See you later then," Catawba said as he walked away.

25

The next morning he found Don pacing outside the front door of the RV. He was shirtless and bug eyed and walking back and forth looking at the ground. Catawba stood there silently and didn't move.

"What do you know about Japanese bushes?"

"Not a damn thing Don."

"See, I called the tree nursery in town a few days back and had them order me a couple. Janice has taken the car so I need you to go get them for me. I've already paid for them so you just have to sign the slip and bring them back. Do you think you can do that for me?"

"Are you feeling alright man?"

"What do you mean?"

"I mean you seem a little off this morning."

"Catawba," he said listlessly, "Janice is gone for good this time. Do you want to help me or not?"

"Sure I'll go get the bushes for you. Just give me the directions and some gas money if you can spare it."

Don nodded at him and walked to the door of the RV and disappeared inside. Catawba took off for his house. He went inside, grabbed his keys, and came back out and met Don in the driveway. He handed him a small slip of paper and a baby food jar filled with nickels. Catawba looked at the items and back at Don.

"I shall return."

He walked over to his car and left. He followed the directions down to the other side of the county. He pulled up in front of a small dilapidated greenhouse and got out. He walked inside and found a small boned man walking amongst the flowers with a waterhose.

"Hey," he called out.

"What do you want?"

"I was sent down here by a man named Don to get some bushes."

The man walked over to the spigot tap and cut the water off. He sat the hose on the ground and went to a desk against the wall. He flipped open a three ring binder and began studying the names.

"What's his name again?"

"Don but I don't know his last name. He lives up at the lake and drives an old Mercedes. He said he already paid you for them."

"Oh yeah I know that weirdo," the man said as he slammed the binder shut. "He never paid me for 'em and I ordered 'em just for him. Tell him he is getting 'em for free as long as he promises to never come back here."

The man walked over and got three small pots of sickly looking purple bushes. He followed Catawba outside and put them in the backseat of the car. Then he dusted off his hands as he walked away. Catawba watched him for a moment and then got in the car and left.

He pulled into the driveway and got the bushes out. He carried them to the front door of the RV and sat them on the ground. He knocked on the door but no one answered and nothing moved inside. He sighed and walked back to his house.

Late in the afternoon he went outside to get his mail. As he started down the driveway he heard a shout and looked over to see Don kicking the bushes across the dirt.

"What in the shit is wrong with you now?"

"Catawba I know you went and bought pot with that jar of change," Don yelled out as he walked toward the property line. "Do you have any idea what I'm going to do when I catch your ass?"

"NOTHING," he shouted at the top of his lungs. "You're going to do absolutely nothing. You're a miserable old dopehead and half crazy, and you better not come over here either, or I'll call the law and tell them to put your ass in a cage down there at the mental hospital."

Don stopped in his tracks and looked blankly at his neighbor. He turned around and hurried back to the RV and went inside. Catawba went on and checked his mail. He walked back up the driveway slowly waiting for something to happen but nothing did. There were no sounds or movement. He went inside his house and didn't think about it again.

A few days later he went outside to leave and saw that the RV was gone. He walked over to the abandoned homestead and looked around. There was nothing left except for the logs and a few neglected flowers. He took a deep breath, smiled, and turned around and headed for his car to leave.

He pulled up behind his grandfather's house and got out. He walked through the backdoor to find the old man sitting at the kitchen table sorting through a collection of doilies. He walked to the head of the table, pulled a chair out, and sat down.

"What do you have those old things out for?"

"Oh, I'm going to go around and put them out. I want to make the house presentable for when she comes to stay."

"Pop," he said calmly, "I want you to look at me."

"What Catawba?"

"When who comes to stay ?"

145

"My sister Dorothy. I called up to Baltimore the other day and asked her to move down here and take care of me. She said she would."

"You're full of yourself. Your sister isn't going to move in with you. How is she going to get down here? Drive? She's almost ninety years old."

"You'll see."

"Good luck to all parties concerned. You guys are not going to fight and drag me into the middle of it."

"We never fight. We get along great."

"I have no idea what goes on with you anymore," he said as he stood up and looked around.

"When are you going to the grocery store again?"

" Tomorrow and you go to the VA hospital Monday."

"Make a list of stuff I need then."

Catawba got a little scrap of paper off the counter and started. He went around to the cabinets and checked in the refrigerator. A time or two his grandfather named some item foreign to his digestive system. He checked and filled up his grandfather's pill trays and sought out and found the cat asleep under the bed. As he walked back to the kitchen table he folded up the little scrap and stuck it in the front pocket of his hiking shorts.

"Oh yeah I almost forgot," his grandfather said as he rubbed his head.

"What?"

"I want some wild wineberries. Like the ones you got me last year."

"Do you know where those come from?"

"Yes, you got them for me."

"No. I mean do you know where I picked them at ?"

"Where?"

"At the bottom of one of the earthen dams. The same dam the cop picked me up on a few days back. The only reason I found them last year was because I got lost in the woods and I'm not doing that again. The only other way to get them is to go down the face of the dam and then try to work my way through a steep ravine of kudzu."

"Well just get me a few then."

146

He frowned at his grandfather and headed for the backdoor. He went outside, got in his car, and drove home without delay. He parked beside the front porch and got out. He went inside and searched around until he found a small plastic bag in a kitchen drawer. He folded it up, slid it in his back pocket, and went back out the front door. He walked over to the porch column and grabbed his bicycle helmet. He donned it, cinched the chin strap tight, and grabbed the handlebars. He pushed the bike off the porch and down to the end of the driveway. He let a car pass, then he hopped on and began pedaling.

He had sweated through his shirt by the time he got to the end of the road and several passing cars had honked in anger. He issued one finger salutes in return and zipped through the stop sign without looking both ways. He cut onto the dam road and began to coast.

When he got to the start of the first earthen dam his legs were beginning to cramp. He stopped in the middle of the road and climbed off. He picked the bicycle up and sat it over the guardrail and into the grass. He unsnapped his helmet and dropped it on top of the bike. He looked down the steep grassy grade of the dam and gritted his teeth. He stepped over the guardrail and sat down in the grass and tried to slide but it held tight like velcro and he didn't move. Then he eased himself up and started a slow descent of wide and measured steps.

He stopped when he reached the bottom of the dam and looked out at the denuded landscape. The power company had devoured all the lumber below the dam and the briar patch in front of him lay dead from industrial herbicides. He sighed and began walking across the dead bramble. The birds were silent and the only noise he heard was the sound of muffled and distant voices to his front. A time or two he slowed to a crawl and looked around to see if anyone was watching him but no one was.

After a few minutes he reached the edge of the ravine. He stopped and looked around. The pine trees on the far side had bright orange flagging tied around their trunks and the thick blooming kudzu below him teemed with bees. He could

147

not see the ground until the small narrow strip of bottomland a hundred yards beneath. He wiped the sweat out of his eyes and started down the slope.

The first steps were easy as the tender young sprouts collapsed without protest and the fragrant grapish aroma wafted up from the blooms. He used big leaves as handholds and stumbled little until he reached the thick mature vines which would not give to his body weight. He found himself crotch deep and unable to move as the pollinating bees whizzed by his head.

He raised his left foot high and sat it down beside his right foot. Then he lowered his body down through the vines until he was submerged in the foliage. He maneuvered his torso around and started a slow and laborious army crawl down the steep slope.

At last his forearms settled upon the flat cool earth. He worked his body free and stood up and looked out at the smorgasbord in front of him. He smiled and started picking and eating berries as fast as his hands could work.

He had devoured a dozen handfuls when he heard a voice coming from above him at the pine trees. He stopped and looked up but saw nothing. He reached into his back pocket for the bag but it was gone. He turned around and looked at the kudzu embankment but didn't see it there either. He walked over and stuck his head into the hole he had shimmied out but it wasn't there. He stood up and looked back around at the bushes and berries. Just my luck, he thought.

Two loud voices came from overhead and he leaped up on the bank and buried himself into the sea of green. He worked himself around until he was on his back beneath the dense foliage.

"Let's cut this big one and call it a day," said an unseen voice.

"Sounds like a winner," replied someone else.

He heard a chainsaw crank followed by the sound of sawing. His face changed color as he tried to force his body up but the vines held tight. He grabbed and pulled and yanked until at last his head was protruding out of the green matting but the only thing he saw was the crown of a large pine tree as it fell toward him. He tensed up, put his hand over his face, and awaited his destiny.

He came to as the light of the day was start ing to wane. His head pounded and his face felt like it had been melted. He worked his hands up until they were above him. He grabbed onto a thick vine and pulled. His body moved little at first but finally he broke free. He turned over onto his belly and began crawling up the side of the slope. Halfway up his shorts became snagged on some unknown protrusion. He tried to work himself free but eventually he gave up and unbuttoned them. He slid out of his shorts and continued crawling up the ravine.

After an hour he reached the top. He prised himself up from the kudzu and dusted the dirt off his bare rear. Then he reached up and touched his face. Numbness mixed with dirt and dried blood. He looked up at the darkening sky to see a wedge of Canadian geese going by honking loudly to each other. He looked back down at the earth in front of him and took off in a brisk trot across the bramble patch.

When he got to the base of the dam he looked up at the road but no cars passed and the land stood silent. He heard a loud crack of thunder over the lake and he took off up the side of the dam using grass stems and dirt clods as climbing implements. When he reached his bicycle he stripped off his t-shirt and fashioned himself a makeshift loincloth. He cinched it tight around his naked parts and donned his helmet. Then he picked up his bicycle and sat it over the guardrail. He hopped on and started pedaling just as the bottom fell out of the sky.

He was soaked to the core by the time he got home. He leaned his bicycle against the porch column and stripped off his shoes and socks at the door. He went inside and headed for the kitchen. He let the shirt drop from around his waist and had a big glass of cold water. He went to the bathroom and looked at his lacerated face in the mirror. He grabbed a hand towel and doused it with peroxide and sat down on the toilet and held the towel against his face.

After a few minutes he let the towel drop to the floor. He stood up and reached into the shower and turned the water to scalding hot. He took a deep breath and stepped under the falling water and screamed with all his might as the water coursed over his open wounds. Then he leaned against the wall watching as the bottom of the shower turned a pale cherry red.

When all the hot water was exhausted he got out of the shower. He wrapped a towel around his waist and staggered to his bed. He collapsed onto the comforter and rolled over onto his side and fell into a deep sleep of distorted dreams where everything seemed to be falling.

26

He woke up at noon the following day. He wheeled his body around and sat on the edge of the bed and touched his swollen face. He sighed and got up and went to the kitchen and turned on the coffee pot. He swallowed a handful of aspirins as he dialed his grandfather's number. The line was busy so he hung up the phone. He picked up the soiled shirt off the floor and threw it away. He poured himself a cup of coffee and then chugged it without breathing. He sat the cup down in the sink and went to get dressed.

The cotton shirt felt like sandpaper against his face as he slid it on. He put on clean shorts and fished an old pair of shoes out from under the bed. He laced them to his feet and stood up. He grabbed his keys and wallet and headed for the backdoor.

He pulled up at the farmers market but the place was empty. He got out and looked around. At the last booth on the end he saw a man in bib overalls loading up his goods in the back of a truck. He took off in a brisk walk toward him.

"Excuse me sir," he said as he got close, "where is everyone?"

"It ended an hour ago. Don't you own a watch?"

"Ah damn it to hell."

"Don't cuss young man . The almighty wouldn't like it. What was it you were in the market for? I might still have it yet."

"Goat cheese."

The farmer stared at him for a moment and continued loading his truck.

"Sir, do you have any?"

"Nah, I ain't got no goat cheese and I don't intend on selling any of that nonsense either. I got a pint jar of wildflower honey I'll let you get."

"I'll take it. I haven't had any wildflower honey since I was a kid."

"And why is that?"

"My grandfather got rid of his beehives years ago."

"Why did he do that?"

"I guess he just got too old to mess around with them."

"It'll be eight dollars then."

Catawba opened his wallet, dug the money out, and sat it down on the empty table top. The farmer looked at the money and began rooting around in the back of his truck. He brought out a glass jar filled with golden liquid and a wedge of honeycomb. He handed it to him and studied his face.

"If you don't mind me asking son what happened to your head?"

"I was out in the woods picking berries when a logger cut a pine tree down on top of me. It just seems like everything is starting to go to hell around here."

"Don't cuss young man . You're from here too I reckon?"

"Yeah, I'm from here."

"What do you do for an occupation?"

"Nothing I can brag about. I'm like everyone else around here. I scrape by the best I can and get the occasional lucky break."

"And say you've worked bees before?"

"I know how to work bees and milk cows and use a hoe."

"Son, my name is Damon," the farmer said as he worked a scrap of paper and pencil nub from his breast pocket, "and I want you to write down your name and address. I may come get you going on next week to help me on my farm. I don't have a phone so I'll send my man to come get you. His name is Nehemiah."

151

Catawba took the paper and pencil nub and wrote out his address. He examined it for a moment and then handed it back to him.

"That's my address and my name is Catawba Fox."

"That's a most unusual name. Is it Christian?"

"It's as Christian as any other name under the firmament."

The man nodded and offered his hand and they shook. Then they stood there for a moment looking at one another before each man turned and went their own way.

Catawba walked back to his car and got in. He drove over to the grocery store and parked. He got out, took two steps, and kicked the curb. Then he took off walking quickly. He went through the double doors, grabbed a shopping cart, and began going down the aisles as he tried to remember what his grandfather needed. He caught other shoppers whispering and pointing at his face as he went along but he didn't say a word to anyone. He went up to the front and paid and pushed the cart outside. He put the groceries in the backseat, shoved the cart out of the way, and got inside. He drove up the road to his grandfather's house as the heat rose from atop the asphalt and the sky threatened rain.

He stopped at the end of the driveway and checked the mail. The neighbor waved to him from her porch and he waved back without much emotion. He started to walk over to her house but she retreated back inside and slammed the door with much heft. He stood there looking at her house for a moment before turning around and going back to his car. He drove up the driveway and parked around back and got out. He got the grocery bags from behind the seat and shut the door. He turned around to see his grandfather standing outside watching him.

"My god Catawba what happened to your face."

"I'll tell you in a minute," he replied as he headed for the backdoor.

He carried the groceries inside the house and took them to the kitchen. He sat them down on the countertop and started fishing stuff out of the bags.

"Don't ever ask me to do something like that again."

"Do what?"

"Go pick berries for you. Everything around here is a damn curse. Fonta Flora, Lake Linville, they're all a damn curse."

"What happened?"

"A logger cut a tree into the gully. The very gully I was trying to pick your berries in but it doesn't matter. I lost the bag I was going to put them in. Then I lost my damn shorts crawling back up the hill through the kudzu. I lose my mind with every day that passes here in this hell. I can't keep a job. I don't have any friends anymore and now going outside isn't even safe to do."

His grandfather went to say something but stopped as Catawba went storming through the house and out onto the porch. He stood there for a minute and then began putting up the groceries in the quietude of the cool kitchen.

When he finished he walked through the house and looked out the screen door. His grandson was sitting on the swing with his eyes closed and his hands palm up as if he were praying. He eased himself out the door and sat down in the rocking chair. Catawba came to and opened his eyes and looked at him.

"Tough day?"

"Tough life. Some guy at the farmers market said he might get me to help him work his fields next week, but I don't want to end up as some destitute field hand with arthritis and a bad back, but that seems to be the normal pattern for this area."

"That is the reason I became a plumber after the war. I don't think I could have handled working in a plant or being in a field."

"Was that what you wanted to do? Be a plumber?"

"Lord no, I never wanted to do much of anything but we all have to do something. I didn't like it at first what with the basements and long hours. Many days I would come home looking like a kid who'd been playing in a mud puddle but after a while I just gave up. See Catawba you can't paddle against the current forever. Sooner or later you just have to resign yourself to destiny."

"What do you mean?"

"You always doubt yourself. You halfass everything you touch and it shows. Sabotaging your jobs and running away from schools. That is nothing more than you paddling against the current. When my sister moves in with…."

"She's not moving in with you."

"Shut up, when my sister moves in with me I want you to drive to the mountains and sit down and think about everything."

"What do you mean by that? Think about everything?"

"Go do what it is you've always wanted to do."

"What does that mean?"

"You'll figure it out when you get your head right," the old man said as he stood up.

Catawba went to speak but stopped as his grandfather opened the screen door and disappeared back inside. He leaned back in the porch swing and looked out over the parched grass as a crow called out near the woodline.

After a long time had passed he got up and went inside the house. His grandfather was lying on the couch looking up at the ceiling. He gave Catawba a farewell nod as he walked through the living room and headed for the backdoor. He got in his car and drove home as multitudes of vehicles pulled their boats back to the city. He cut into his driveway and got out. He walked down to the mailbox but found nothing. He grabbed his groceries and went inside the house and put them up. He went to his desk and sat down. He tried to type but the words wouldn't come to him. When the daylight outside died away he got up and went to the bathroom and dabbed ointment on his face. Then he stood there looking at his swollen and wounded face in the mirror as the clock on the wall ticked away a slow cadence of unknown rectitude.

27

H e was standing at his desk the next day when he heard someone knocking at the front door. Bam. Bam. Bam. He walked to the side window and looked outside but didn't see anything. He crept to the front door, took a deep breath, and yanked it open to find a familiar face standing there with a yellow daffodil behind her ear.

"Nevena? I didn't expect…"

"I thought you were a park ranger Catawba."

"They fired me for incompetence and I'm not going back to class either."

"I know. They told me you were canned when I went to the park office but a man named Vance gave me your address."

"That was nice of him."

"And last week someone came into class and talked to us about you. They said you were trouble. I didn't believe them though. Is this a bad time?"

"No, of course not. I was just at my desk gathering up all the pages I have typed out over the last few weeks. Come in."

She walked through the door and down the hallway and stopped. He walked past her and went back to his desk.

"See," he said as he picked up a stack of paper, "I've typed out everything that's happened to me over the last few weeks. I'm thinking of turning it into a book."

"Am I in the book?"

"Do you want to be?"

"It doesn't matter. Just make sure I'm the heroine that saves the day."

"Yeah right. That would be like pulling a porcupine out of a pillow."

"Don't you mean pulling a rabbit out of a hat?

"Close enough."

She snickered and walked over to the typewriter and pecked a couple of keys. Then she turned around and looked at him for a moment and headed for the front door.

"You coming," she called from the front porch.

"I'm right behind you."

He walked out onto the porch and pulled the front door shut and followed her down the steps and to her car at the end of the driveway.

"Where are we going?"

"You told me you would tell me about this area and I want to hear about it. Just tell me where to drive."

"Alright," he said as he opened the car door, "let's go see Fonta Flora from the clouds."

They climbed inside and shut their doors. She cranked the car and he pointed down the road. She pulled out behind a truck towing a boat and they headed off. When they got to the end of the road he pointed to the left. She turned and they headed out over the first earthen dam.

"This is gorgeous Catawba," she said as she looked out her window at the lake and mountains.

"Yes it is. The lake was manmade about a hundred years ago. The power company built it for hydroelectric power but now their only concern is selling off the remaining land for houses and harvesting the timber."

They drove on, going over the spillway bridge, and across the power generation dam with him pointing stuff out and her trying to take it all in. When they got to the end of the road he told her to turn left. She consented and they headed out into the hinterlands of Lake Lineville. They had traveled a few miles when she looked over at him.

"I hope it is not impolite to ask but what happened to your face."

"A tree was cut on top of me while I was out picking berries."

"Oh I'm sorry."

"It's alright. I'll heal like I always do."

"Where are you taking me?"

"We are going up here to Wolf Pit Road and hike to the top of Table Rock Mountain."

She nodded and they drove on as the road began to skirt the east side of the lake. They went past a small marina and he told her to take the next right. She slowed down and cut off onto a rutted out gravel road. Then she looked over at him and spoke.

"Are there any wolves up here on this road?"

"Not anymore. When I was a child I was told that this was where they killed the last wolf in the area. They dug a deep pit and when the poor creature got trapped in it they shot it. I don't even know if the story is true but that's how the story goes."

"Why did they shoot the wolf?"

"To tell you the truth I don't know. Maybe it was harassing the livestock or maybe they just got sick of it running free but it doesn't matter at the end of the day because once you destroy something it's gone forever."

"Oh."

They bounced up the road through potholes and across exposed rocks until they got to the end. The parking lot was choked with vehicles and she eased her car off the road and into the weeds. They looked at each other for a moment and then got out and shut their doors. He reached down and snugged up the laces on his hiking shoes while she walked over to the forest service information board.

"It says there are peregrine falcons up there," she called out over her shoulder.

"Yeah," he said as he walked up beside her, "it says that but I've never seen them."

"Lead the way," she said as she turned to him.

He nodded and they took off walking. The first section of the trail was a miry mess from recent rains and the little rivulets trickled with water as they swept around the big loose rocks. They hiked on for twenty minutes until they ran into a small knot of talkative nature enthusiasts descending the mountain. They moved to the side of the trail and stood by a scraggly balsam tree as they waited for the group to pass.

"Do you come up here much?" she asked after the last person went by.

"I used to," he replied as he stepped back on the trail, "but then it became a hassle with all the people pouring in from out of state just for the photography.'

They hiked on with Lake Linville and Fonta Flora starting to resemble a child's playset sprawled out on a carpet of green. Close to the summit they stopped to catch their breath. She looked out at the valley below and he looked over at her.

"Are you ready?" he asked after a few minutes. "We're almost at the top."

"Let's do this."

They took off again, stepping on and over large granite rocks and looking around at the windswept coniferous trees.

Near the top they came upon a large swath of charred brush from a recent fire and he slowed down and looked at her.

"Most of the forest fires around here are caused by humans but I don't think they care as long as they get their photos and have their fun."

"Oh," she replied.

He wiped the sweat from his forehead and started hiking faster with her right behind him. In no time at all they were standing on the flat rocky top of the mountain looking out over the lake and city.

"I never would have thought it looked like this," she said as she tried to take it all in. "It all looks so quaint and innocent from up here."

"I know what you mean but when you go down there it is a congested nightmare. I remember when I was a kid it was just a normal small town but those days are long gone it seems. So I spend a lot of my time trying to remember the way things were and trying to put it all back together again but it doesn't work out."

"I don't understand. What are you trying to put back together? Your childhood?"

"Not my childhood but my youth. I don't remember most of their names but I can see their smiling faces and hear their mellifluous voices. Sometimes I can see everything clear as day. Their faces are like the little rays of sunshine that come down through the treetops when you're out walking in the woods. You turn around and try to snatch them out of the air but nothing happens. You just end up staring at an empty hand and being haunted by another perfect moment lost to eternity. And then it really hits you."

"What hits you?"

"You have to change with the times or live the rest of your life in torment."

"Oh," she said, "it's not that bad. Everyone can change. Besides, I like this place. It reminds me of the country I come from. It's so green and hilly and luscious."

"It sure is. Centuries ago an English explorer called this part of the country the goodliest soil under the cope of heaven."

"Really?"

"Yes."

"That's beautiful."

"Yes it is, but I'm not sure what he would say about it today now that everything likable and decent has been destroyed."

"What? What destroyed it?"

"It was destroyed when they started building stripmalls, fast food chains, coffee shops, robotics schools, hipster beer breweries, fitness studios and all that other useless nonsense people think they need to be happy. Then you throw in a million different clowns all trying to..."

He stopped talking and watched as she took off walking back down the trail.

"Where are you going?" he called out.

"I own the fitness studio in town you idiot," she called back fiercely.

He went to say something but stopped. Instead he sat down on the rocky surface and watched as she walked down the trail and disappeared out of sight.

A few hours later he wiped the salty moisture from his eyes and stood up and walked over to a laurel bush and made water behind it. When he finished he headed to the otherside of the summit. He stopped a few feet from the ledge and looked down into the gorge. The Linville River looked like a silvery snake slithering through thick grass as it headed towards the lake. He heard a screechy call coming from behind him and turned around to see a peregrine falcon sitting on a gnarled log. The bird's yellow legs and checkered chest feathers shone brightly in the summer sun. The bird hopped down and bounced along the rocky top until it was at his feet. He looked down at the falcon and the falcon looked up at him. He smiled as the bird began beating its wings quickly. It hopped to the very edge of the ledge, looked back at him, and jumped. The bird shot down into the gorge like a primitive missile, then it turned and glided alongside the river until it disappeared out of sight.

Catawba felt a rush of cool air blow across his face. He took a deep breath and reached down and recinched his laces and stood back up. He turned around and started back down the mountain at an easy pace, stopping to look at anything and everything that caught his eye. A time or two he nodded to people who were hiking up to the summit. He got back to the parking lot just as the light of the day was beginning to die. He found an older gentleman sitting on the tailgate of a truck changing his shoes.

"Excuse me sir," he said.

"Yes?"

"I got stranded here. I live on the other side of the lake close to the park."

"Ok."

"Is there any way you could drop me off there if you're heading that way?"

"I don't see a problem with that," the man said as stood up. "Hop in the passenger's side seat and I'll take you home before it gets dark."

He walked over and got in the truck. He buckled his seatbelt and sat there staring through the windshield. The man climbed inside and cranked the engine and off they went. They reached the main highway just as total darkness fell upon the land. The man drove quickly as he told Catawba about his hiking exploits and life. Catawba sat there motionless, listening and answering with the occasional monosyllable.

The man let him out at the bottom of his driveway, told him goodbye and good luck, and drove on. He walked up the gravel and disappeared through the front door. He staggered through the house and to his bed where he collapsed in a wave of neurasthenia.

28

The next morning he walked through the backdoor of his grandfather's house and stopped. The old man was sitting at the table with a stack of photographs in front of him. The air conditioner was running and the house felt welcoming.

"Your face is starting to look a little better," the old man said sprightly.

160

"The swelling has gone down some. Are you ready to go?"

"Where are we going today? I forgot."

"I'm taking you up the mountain to your doctor's appointment."

"Well let me lock up the front door then."

His grandfather stood up slowly, grabbed his walking stick, and took off through the house. Catawba walked over to the table and looked at the old photographs. They were black and white and several of them faded beyond all recognition. After a few minutes his grandfather came back into the kitchen and grabbed his hat off the coat rack.

"You see those pictures there?"

"I glanced at them."

"Those are from when I was a kid in the forties. I got them out so I would be ready."

"That's good I guess," he said as he turned around and looked at him. "Are you going to take your walker or the walking stick?"

"I'll just take this walking stick. I'm not that hobbled up today."

"Well let's get going before the traffic gets heavy on the interstate."

He walked through the kitchen and out the backdoor with his grandfather following behind him. They got in the car together and buckled up.

"Did you forget to lock the backdoor?"

"No, I meant to leave it unlocked."

"Well it's your house."

Catawba put the car in gear and they left. He went over to the interstate and took the westbound lane. When he got up to speed he looked over at his grandfather.

"The mountains always seem to sparkle in the summertime."

"Yeah, they sure do, but I'll just be glad to get back home."

"Don't worry it won't take that long with the conveyor belt healthcare at the VA. I want to go back with you this time. I want to ask your doctor some questions."

"I don't know why. I'm as fit as a fiddle."

"Well let's just see what the doctor says."

Catawba looked back at the road and picked up more speed. An hour later he turned off the interstate and cut onto the main road that led to the hospital.

"I'm going to let you out at the front door. You just wait right there while I go park the car and we'll go back to the doctor's offices together."

"Okay," his grandfather replied.

A few minutes later he cut off the main highway and onto the grounds of the VA hospital. He drove past the guidons and statutes and circled around to the front door where an uniformed greeter stood fielding questions at a podium.

"Go stand next to the greeter until I get back."

"Okay."

His grandfather opened the door, grabbed his walking stick, and took off. Catawba watched him for a second and then drove over to the big parking lot at the side of the building. He found an empty space beneath a maple tree and parked. He got out and took off quickly back to the front doors. When he got there he didn't see his grandfather.

"Hey," he said to the greeter, "did my grandfather already go in?"

The greeter shrugged his shoulders so he went inside. He walked through the lobby, past the various murals, and headed for the doctor's offices in the back of the hospital. Throngs of older men stood around swapping war stories with their buddies while the intercom blared out names overhead.

When he got to the primary care offices the waiting room was full but he didn't see his grandfather. He went up to the receptionist's window and stood.

"May I help you sir?"

"Uh yes, I was wondering if my grandfather has checked in already."

"What is his name?"

He told her.

"You just missed him. They've already taken him back."

"I need to go back there with him. I need to tell the doctor that he is having memory problems."

"I'm sorry sir but protocol for the Department of Veterans Affairs states that only the patient is allowed to go back. You'll just have to wait out here. There's vending machines around the corner if you want to go have a cup of coffee until he comes out."

"Thanks a lot. You've been so helpful."

He took off around the corner and came upon a little room with tables and snack machines. He walked inside and headed for an antique coffee machine against the back wall. He read the instructions and fished the required silver out of his pocket. He put the money in the machine and pushed the button but nothing happened. He pushed it again and the machine made a crackling sound and cut off. He grabbed the top of it with both hands and commenced kicking it.

"Hey there," came a booming voice behind him, "stop that and come over here."

He turned around to see an older man sitting at a table. He walked over to the table and looked at him. He had greying hair and wore thick sunglasses.

"Sit down here young man and tell me what's wrong. I'm one of the trauma counselors here at the hospital."

He consented and sat down. He tapped his fingers on the laminate tabletop and started spewing. He told the man about his grandfather, his misadventures in life, and how he hated what his hometown had become. When he finished the man looked at him without emotion.

"Fonta Flora? I know that area well. See I was born in this state too. When I was a kid my parents took me there many times to see family but that was back before the country tried to destroy itself."

"I don't understand sir."

"I was born back in forty-six after the world war ended. I grew up thinking that surely a new dawn was breaking upon the country but I was wrong, I was so wrong, because this country turned around and tried to kill me."

163

"What do you mean by that? This country tried to kill you?"

"I got drafted into the service and ended up at Khe Sahn."

"Was that a battle during Vietnam?"

"Battle? That was a siege," the man said as he pushed the glasses back on his face. "For seventy-seven days straight our base was assaulted by the North Vietnamese Army and there was never a moment of let up. Constant shelling and mortar fire made our lives a living hell. The planes that delivered the supplies didn't even stop. They just kept rolling down the runway and pushed their cargo off. The Vietnamese soldiers we killed just laid there and rotted in the concertina wire because hell, we couldn't bury them. We just didn't have the time. After a few weeks I got used to smelling those rotting bodies and seeing uniformed skeletons laying around peering at me through empty eye sockets. But then they finally evacuated us. I had so many friends die and get wounded over there but I walked away without even getting a scratch."

"Damn man."

"Yes and damn all those men at the airport when I came back stateside. Their filthy mouths and their spitting filled my heart so much hate. I ended up hating them even more than I hated the Vietnamese."

"What did you do then? When you got back?"

"Oh I took the rest of my combat pay and went out on a drinking spree. I caught a bus down to New Orleans and got a room in a flophouse and two cases of cheap gin. I would drink and I would rage and I would shout at the sky about my terrible lot in life. But then my money started to dwindle and I tried to hitchhike home. I made it a ways but then I got stranded in Valdosta Georgia and spent the last of my money on a big jug of cheap wine. I remember uncapping the jug and having a big drink as the sweat rolled down my stinking body and then nothing. I came to in a hospital there some days later. The doctor said I'd staggered out in front of a car on the edge of town. I had a bad concussion, some broken bones, and I was cut up from head to toe. He said I was lucky to be alive. He told me I ought to do something constructive with my

164

life. So when I got out I called my family and they wired me money for bus fare. I came back home and worked for a while as a dishwasher but that got old quick so I went back to school. I was the first person in my family to graduate from college and now here we are. I've spent the last several decades working here at the VA hospital as a palliative care and trauma counselor. I'm starting to get on in years and I've let so much anger go from my heart but I can't stop thinking that the car that hit me was a sign from God. I think he has to scare you to death sometimes to set you on the straight and narrow."

"I've been scared before too sir, but just not on your level."

"No you haven't son," the man said as he stood up, "not yet and you better pray that it never happens, because if it does, you won't be acting the way you are. Now go back and check on your grandfather. I have to go talk to a man who is dying of pancreatic cancer."

Catawba watched the man as he turned around and walked away. He sat at the table for a long time oblivious to everything around him. Then he got up and headed back. He turned the corner to see his grandfather coming out the door.

"Hey Cat, are you ready to go?"

"Huh?"

"Are you ready to go?"

"Uh."

"I said, are you ready to go home?"

"I think so. I mean…"

"What's wrong with you? You seem bothered by something."

"It's nothing I guess. What did the doctor say?"

"The doctor told me my hip is doing fine," he replied as he hurried past him on his walking stick. "Now let's go home."

"I'm right behind you."

They walked together slowly through the hospital and toward the front door with Catawba keeping his hand slightly off his grandfather's shoulder. When they got to the sliding glass doors Catawba told him to go stand next to the wall while he went to retrieve the car. His grandfather nodded and he took off through the parking lot.

He pulled back around to the front of the hospital and stopped. His grandfather was leaning up against the cement wall talking to a man in scrubs. He motioned with his hand and his grandfather shuffled over and got in.

"Cut that air conditioner down," he said as he shut the door, "I'm freezing."

"It's not on Pop but I wish it was. You just have poor circulation."

"Oh."

"Put your seatbelt on."

"Okay."

Catawba drove around the loop and headed off the grounds of the VA hospital as the incoming traffic sat bumper to bumper. He drove over to the interstate and shot down the entrance ramp. When he got up to speed he looked over at his grandfather. He was fiddling with a slip of paper and muttering under his breath.

"What is that? Is that a note from the doctor?"

"Oh it's just some junk they gave me."

"Well what does it say? Read it off to me?"

His grandfather looked at him, rolled the window down an inch, and fed the paper through the opening. Catawba looked in the rearview window and saw the paper serpentining through the air as it pinballed off car windshields. He squeezed the steering wheel of the car and looked back over at his grandfather.

"Never in my entire life have I seen you litter. Tell me what that paper said. Was it from the doctor?"

"Shut up. It was just junk. I don't have to tell you everything."

"So be it then. Did they give you another appointment in six months?"

There was no reply so he looked back at the road and said no more about it. He drove with the flow of traffic and tried to make small talk as they descended the mountain but to no avail. His grandfather sat in stoic silence looking out the

166

window at the passing farmhouses and fields. The trip back home took close to an hour.

He began to perk up however when they turned into his driveway. Catawba drove up the gravel and around to the back of the house. An antique blue sedan was backed up close to the door but no one was around it. His grandfather punched him in the ribs and got out posthaste. He hurried up to the backdoor and disappeared inside. After a few minutes Catawba got out too and walked to the backdoor and went inside. He walked into the kitchen and stopped.

His grandfather and a willowy woman were sitting at the kitchen table looking at the pictures. She was pointing at various ones and giggling as he told her their significance. Catawba studied her features for a moment, then he cleared his throat and they looked up.

"How've you been Dorothy?"

"Well I'll declare," she said as she stood up, "I haven't seen you since you were a tiny little kid. Do you still ride your bike and play baseball for the school?"

"Of course I do, but that's only when I'm not shooting marbles on the sidewalk."

"Kids never change," she said as she walked over to hug him. "You want me to fix you something to eat?"

"I'm good," he replied as he hugged her tightly. "I'm not really in the mood for food right now. Are you here to stay?"

"Your grandfather needs all the help he can get. What with him being in his eighties now and lame."

"But Aunt Dorothy, you're even older than he is."

"Nonsense. I'm only in my sixties," she replied as she walked back to the table.

"Really? You're only in your sixties huh?"

"Of course I am and I still have all my own teeth."

"Well I stand corrected then."

"Can I get you to do me a favor while I have it on my mind?"

"Sure I will. What is it?"

"Will you go outside and get my things out of the car? I have a surprise for you."

"Okay."

He turned around and walked outside to the car. He opened the back hatch and retrieved two leather suitcases and a small open satchel of towels. He tucked everything under his arms and closed the hatch. He walked back inside and sat the stuff down next to the kitchen table. Then he walked to the living room and sat down on the couch and peered out the front window.

After a few minutes the noise from the kitchen stopped and they filed into the room and sat down too. She pulled a change purse out of her pocket, undid the clasp, and began rummaging around in it. She brought out a crinkled up bill and held it up close to her face. She studied the markings of the bill before reaching over and handing it to him.

"That ten dollars will do you all summer Catawba. You can buy all the ice cream you want now."

"Thank you so much."

He slid the bill into his front pocket and rubbed his sinuses tightly. Then he looked over at his grandfather and stood up.

"Hey Pop."

"What is it?"

"Can I see you in the kitchen for a moment? I need to ask you about my car."

"Okay."

He walked through the house and stopped at the head of the kitchen table. His grandfather followed him to the table, pulled out a chair, and sat down.

"What?"

"Are you sure about this?"

"Sure about what?"

"Her living with you. She seems a little bit senile."

"What makes you think she is senile?"

"She doesn't know how old she is and she thinks I'm a kid even though I'm six foot tall."

"She'll be fine. You and I talked about this. You're free now to go do what you want in life. Go to the mountains, go anywhere, but just go."

"Maybe it's the other way around. Did you ever think about it like that? Maybe I need you more than you need me."

"Nonsense Catawba. Just go and let go. I'll be fine."

He tried to speak but his stomach knotted up and nothing came out. He walked to the backdoor and disappeared outside. He stood there looking up at the trees trying to hear the sounds of songbirds or any birds but heard only the faint whisperings of the wind in the summer heat.

29

A few days later he was standing out on the front porch taping up his cardboard American flag when he heard the sound of brakes in his driveway. He turned around to see a lanky man in overalls stepping out of a beat-up work truck. He sat the tape down on the porch swing and walked over to the steps as the man approached. The man stopped when he got within a few paces of the bottom step and spoke.

"You Catawba?"

"I could be. What do you want?"

"My name's Nehemiah and the reverend said you'd help me rob the honey out of the beehives."

"Reverend?" Catawba asked slowly. "Do you mean Damon from the farmers market?"

"The Honorable Reverend Damon Abfall is the head of Fonta Flora Primitive Holiness Non-Denominational Church of Signs and Wonders."

"Well that's quite the revelation there."

"Oh yes sir, he has revelations all the time about people, places, and things."

"And how long is it going to take to work up the honey?"

"We should be done near suppertime or sometime after."

"Look, I don't have a beekeeper's suit and we never discussed compensation. It was more idle conversation than anything else."

"The reverend doesn't like idleness. Says it ain't Christian. But don't you worry, everything will fall into place as the reverend hath ordained."

169

"I see," Catawba said with a slight grin. "Let me go lock up the house and we'll go down that road together Nehemiah, just like missionaries on a pilgrimage.

"That'll be fine. Just fine."

He walked back up the steps and went inside the house. He went to the backdoor and locked it. He closed the blinds up and headed back to the front porch. He opened the door to find Nehemiah standing on the top step staring at him.

"Is everything alright?" he asked as he pulled the door shut.

He didn't answer as he turned around and walked down the steps and headed for the truck. Catawba watched him for a few seconds before following behind him slowly. He walked down to the end of the driveway and climbed inside the cab of the truck with him. Nehemiah nodded, cranked the engine, and back out into the road.

They drove up the road until they came to the stop sign. Nehemiah looked both ways and cut right. The truck chugged along for many miles until they drew close to the national forest on the north side of the lake. Catawba watched the mountains roll past through the windshield as Nehemiah sat stockstill staring at the road. After an hour they got to a gravel road that disappeared into a grove of poplar trees. Nehemiah downshifted and turned off onto the gravel. They traveled through the forest for a few minutes before coming out in a massive clearing with verdant fields on both sides.

Catawba looked out the side window to see moocows picking grass and bellowing at each other with loud levity. He looked back through the windshield again to see a two story farmhouse quickly approaching; to the right of the house sat a big Dutch style barn with various small dilapidated buildings situated behind it.

Nehemiah cut abruptly through the grass and headed for the barn. He parked in front of the big double doors and they got out together.

"Go to the house and see the reverend," Nehemiah said as he took off toward the barn. "He should be in the front room."

Catawba took off for the house in a fast trot. When he reached the front porch he stopped for a moment before climbing the steps and walking to the screen door. He grabbed the nob and pulled the door open and stepped inside to find the air hot and thick. The reverend was sitting behind a big mahogany desk with his hands on top of his head looking at him.

"Mr. Fox, I hope Nehemiah didn't call on you at a bad time."

"No sir, I was just taping up my Fourth of July flag when he showed up."

"That's good. Your face is looking better I see. Please sit down."

He walked across the room and sat down in a straight back chair facing the desk. He looked around the room and studied the framed photographs from days long past.

"I'm the last of my family," the reverend said as he put his hands down on top of the desk. "After me the line is broken. We're a dying breed."

"I'm the last of my line too. There's not a single thing in this world that lasts forever. Nehemiah says you're a minister."

"Reverend, I prefer reverend. Even though that might be splitting hairs, I just prefer it that way. And where do you stand on the subject of the almighty? Are you churched ?"

"Churched?"

"Is there somewhere you attend on a regular basis?"

"No reverend there's not. I was brought up in a Baptist household. I even went to one of their church schools but I've not crossed the threshold of a church door since I was a teenager. Too many hypocrites fill the pews these days."

"That's not your fault son. The Baptists are a heathenish lot. Very fond of pulling a cork and striking a fiddle, even on Sunday. I'm P rimitive Holiness and I'm proud to say it. You ought to come to my church sometime and join my flock. We have a very beautiful building and an amazing service. "

"No thank you reverend. Ornate buildings and pious platitudes have never done anything to separate the wheat from the tares."

"That's blasphemy," the reverend said as he slapped the top of the desk. "I ought to have Nehemiah drive your ass back home."

"So be it," Catawba said as he stood up.

"No, no, now hold on and sit back down."

He sat back down and looked back across the top of the desk at the reverend.

"I need you to help Nehemiah today and if you do alright maybe this could become some kind of permanent arrangement."

"We never talked about compensation."

"That's because I have yet to see you do the first lick of work. However," he said as he leaned over his desk and looked at a piece of paper, "there is one item we have to clear up first. I went by the sheriff's office at the first of the week and had them look up the legal name you gave me. Do you know what they said?"

"I have no idea sir."

"They said you've had numerous convictions. Everything from public intoxication to disorderly conduct."

"They told you the truth but that was just the waywardness of my misspent youth. Besides, pride and greed and backbiting are all perfectly legal and they've done more damage to this world than any wayward young person."

"The good book doesn't speak highly of mischief son," he said as he looked up from the paper.

"Nor does it speak highly of the judgemental," Catawba responded quickly.

"You have a very interesting interpretation of scripture. Some might call it freethinking."

"To each his own I guess. Look, do you want me to help Nehemiah with the bees?"

"I don't have any other choice it seems. Me and him can't do it alone and you're already here. If you do good I'll let you come back and help us some more but I can already tell you that with a record like yours I won't be able to pay you much of anything."

"And just how much are you going to pay me?"

He told him and told him it was nonnegotiable.

172

"I guess I'll have to take you up on that, but if I work here I'm going to start driving to the farm. I'm not waiting on Nehemiah to pick me up."

"Absolutely not," he said loudly as he stood up. "You're liable to bring a crokersack and try to pilfer a little corn, run it through a still and make a little moonshine."

"I wouldn't do that."

"You might. I've seen it all before son ."

"I'm going to go outside and help Nehemiah now."

"You do that and don't let me catch you idling about, you hear?"

Catawba stood up, turned around, and hurried for the door. He went outside and headed for the barn. Inside he found Nehemiah in a room to the right of the big doors. He was holding a hatchet and looking down at a pile of kindling.

" You ready to do this?"

"Anytime you are. Did you get things squared away with the reverend?"

"I guess we did. He seems like a very strange person."

"We're all weird in our own way," Nehemiah said as he pitched the hatchet on top of the wood. "Now let's go get suited up."

"Alright."

They walked to the back of the barn and went into a small tack room with wall hung tools and cabinets. Nehemiah walked over and opened one of the cabinets and got out two white beekeeper suits and tossed them onto the ground. Then he pulled out an old bee smoker and sat it atop the plank countertop and looked over at Catawba.

"Well put your suit on while I get this thing a-going ."

He nodded and took off his shoes. He climbed into the suit and put his shoes back on as Nehemiah packed cloth strips into the fire chamber. He stood up and watched Nehemiah t ake a small matchbook out of his pocket. He pried one out and struck it against the side of the box. He lit the combustibles, closed the top and squeezed the bellows, causing a plume of smoke to come out the nozzle.

Nehemiah stopped messing with the smoker and grabbed his suit and dressed himself quickly as Catawba stood there in silence. He got gloves out of the cabinet and tossed a pair over. They put them on and then took turns zipping up the back of each other's suits. Then reached back into the cabinet and took out two bee veils and handed one over to Catawba. They put them on and looked at one another.

"I want you to grab the wheelbarrow that is propped up outside the barn. I'll crack open the hives and smoke the bees and take out the honey frames. You just put the frames in the wheelbarrow and when you get enough roll 'em up there to the porch. Give them to the reverend and he'll do the rest."

"Okay."

Nehemiah picked up the smoker and they took off out of the barn in a slow trot. Catawba grabbed the wheelbarrow from against the side of the barn and started pushing it across the grass toward the apiary a hundred yards away.

When he got there he sat the wheelbarrow down next to the end hive. Nehemiah looked at the hive for a few seconds, sat the smoker on the ground, and started walking back towards the barn.

"I forgot my handtools," he called out over his shoulder.

He came back quickly bearing a hand brush and putty knife. He sat the brush down in the wheelbarrow and lifted the outer cover from atop the hive. He took the putty knife and prised up the inner cover revealing a buzzing mass of bees. He picked up the smoker and worked the bellows. A gentle ribbon of smoke came out and engulfed the top of the honey frames inside the box. Then he sat the smoker down and grabbed the first frame of honey. He pulled it out slowly, looking at the swollen and golden colored honeycomb.

"That'll go good on a biscuit won't it?"

"Honey goes on good on anything."

He smiled and began gently brushing the bees off the rack. He worked the hive slowly, sitting the frames inside the wheelbarrow while Catawba stood there watching. He repeated the process through three hives without stopping. Then he told Catawba to take it to the front porch of the house. He nodded and grabbed the handles of the wheelbarrow and lifted. The load was heavy and he hemorrhaged sweat as he started toward the house with a retinue of bees following him.

He halted the wheelbarrow in front of the porch steps and eased it down. Newspapers were laid out across the porch leading up to a stainless steel honey extractor. The reverend opened the screen door and stepped outside. He looked down at the wheelbarrow and Catawba.

"Sit the frames down on the newspaper and space them out. I'm going to start putting them in the extractor and spinning them out."

"Yes sir."

He began grabbing frames and sitting them up on the porch as the reverend watched with glee. When he finished he grabbed the handles of the wheelbarrow and headed back. As soon as he cleared the barn he saw Nehemiah looking under the covers of the other hives. He turned his way when he heard the wheelbarrow approaching.

"We've got ten more hives. I checked them out while you was up there."

"Okay," he replied.

They repeated the process and in a few hours the job was done and the porch was full of honey frames.

"Just lean the wheelbarrow back up against the barn," the reverend said as Catawba sat the last frame down.

"Yes sir."

He pushed the wheelbarrow back to the side of the barn and propped it up against the wall. He walked back inside and found Nehemiah disrobing and covered in sweat. Catawba took off his veil, sat it on the ground, and wiped the sweat from his eyes. He kicked off his shoes and stripped off the beekeeper's suit.

"Why does stuff like this always have to be done on the hottest days of the year?"

"It's July. It's always hot," Nehemiah replied without emotion.

He put his shoes back on, gathered up the paraphernalia in his arms, and carried it back to the tack room. He sat it down on the countertop and walked back to Nehemiah.

"I guess we're done now."

"Done? We've got to help the reverend spin it out," Nehemiah said as he picked up his suit.

He carried his stuff back to the tack room and returned after a few minutes. Then he took off walking for the house with Catawba in tow. They walked up on the porch together as the reverend sat there quietly turning the handle on the extractor.

"You boys take over. I have to run into town."

"Sure thing," Nehemiah said as he headed for the chair.

The reverend got up and went inside the house and came back out carrying a big metal trash can. He handed it to Catawba and pointed at the floor of the porch.

"Use it to sit on."

He turned it upside down and placed it next to the extractor. He sat down on it as the reverend took off for the truck next to the barn.

"Is there somewhere I could get a drink of water?"

Nehemiah looked over at him and nodded his head. He got up and went inside the house. He came back out with a mason jar filled with water and handed it to him. Catawba took a big drink of the tepid water and wiped his mouth.

"Do you want some Nehemiah?"

"Nah, I'm good for now. I had a glass inside."

He put the jar between his knees and looked around at the bees. Some buzzed through the air with frantic intentions while others crawled sluggishly about on the unspun frames.

"Tell me when you want me to take over."

"I'll do it for now. I can do it faster than you can."

"Okay then."

He sat there watching Nehemiah and taking small swigs from the jar. After a few minutes he sat the jar down on the floor boards and looked out at the fields and cows and outbuildings.

"How do you get to work? I don't see another car anywhere."

"I live here."

"You live here?"

"I live," Nehemiah said as he raised his finger and pointed, "right out there in that little tobacco shack near the woods."

"Wow. Have you always lived here with the reverend?"

"Heavens no. I used to work at a factory until they closed it down. Then I clerked at the feed store in town for nearly ten years but they had to close it too when they started raising the rent. The reverend was a regular customer there and he offered to let me stay here and work for my keep."

"I know all about the feed store Nehemiah. I went by there a few weeks ago and they were cleaning it out. They opened a fitness studio in it."

"What's a fitness studio and what do people do there?"

"A fitness studio is where people go to workout. People who have no concept of work to begin with."

Nehemiah stopped cranking and stood up. He took a deep breath and stared at Catawba.

"You spin a little while. I need to go get some air."

"Okay."

He slid over to the chair and grabbed the handle and began cranking away. Nehemiah walked off the porch and toward the cows in the field. He trotted along looking at the ground and kicking at little rocks and mounds of dirt. After a while Catawba checked the frames and switched them out. He was cranking away when Nehemiah walked back up on the porch.

"I'm sorry I walked away and left you to do it alone."

"No, it's my fault. I shouldn't have told you about that but that's everywhere around here. Nothing will be left untouched when those immoral people get done. You and I are just two deer caught in the headlights of change."

"Maybe we can show them a better way to live."

"I don't think so. They wouldn't understand the concept. They're too far gone."

"They're knee deep in with the devil's handiwork is that it?"

"No, not that. At least I don't think so. The way I see it, the measure of a man's morality is how he treats others when he has more power and position than they do."

177

"I still don't understand. If it's not the devil then what is it?"

"The corruption of ego. The most wicked people in the world are the people who go around doing evil but yet firmly believe they are doing good. Evil can deceive the person, but it cannot get the person to deceive themselves. That's where the corrupted ego comes in."

"I never thought about it like that. You know you're very smart."

"I don't know about that. Sooner or later intelligence has to give way to wisdom otherwise what's the point?"

"That's true."

"Here," Catawba said as he stood up, "relieve me for a while. My arm is getting tired."

"Sure."

They traded places on the porch and sat back down. Catawba looked out across the farm. The cows hung together in small groups near hayricks and the tiny buildings seemed listless in the late afternoon heat. A small stand of weathered corn sat out by itself beyond the apiary. Nehemiah switched the frames out several more times and cranked the handle with celerity. He stood up when he was done, lifted the cover, and looked inside the extractor.

"That'll do her. I bet there's close to a hundred pounds of honey in the bottom of this machine."

"Are we going to put it in jars now?"

"No, we'll let it drain down overnight."

"Well what do we do now? He's still gone in the truck."

"We'll go lean these sticky frames up against the back of the barn and let the bees clean up what's left."

"Okay."

Catawba started picking up the frames and flicking off the wayward bees as he went. Nehemiah joined him and after several trips they found themselves standing in the shade behind the big barn.

"I'm done for the day," Nehemiah said as he looked out towards the shack. "I'm beat."

"Well how do I get home then?"

"Don't worry we'll finish up in the morning. Besides I'm not sure how long the reverend intends on being gone this evening."

Nehemiah took off walking towards the shack as Catawba stood stockstill watching him. "Damn it," he whispered. He turned around and walked back to the porch and got the quart jar of water. He drained the remnants in one swallow and took off for the shack too.

When he got there he saw that the tobacco shack was doorless and dirt floored. Nehemiah was laying on a massive quilt in the middle of dirt looking up at the exposed roof beams.

"Take your shoes off and rest a spell."

Catawba dropped the jar by the doorframe and eased himself down onto the dirt against the protests of his tired body. Nehemiah raised his head up and watched him with an amused look on his face.

"It takes some getting used. Farm work is a lot different from stores and factories."

"That's the truth."

"I'll get us up some water and food for supper in a little bit. I just want to cool down for now."

"That's fine by me," Catawba said. "I was thinking as I walked out here that I didn't get stung once today."

"I've never been stung. I was always told that bees won't sting a Melungeon. Maybe that's why."

"I'm not sure bees understand the concept of ancestry but I'll ask one the next chance I get."

Nehemiah chuckled as he rolled over on his side. Catawba scooted around and worked his body down against the cool earth. Then he put his hands under his head and closed his eyes.

When he came to, he was alone. He sat up and leaned forward and looked outside. Nehemiah was walking toward the cabin carrying a large wicker basket in both hands. He stood up and stepped out the door.

"Come take this while I go back and get us some water."

"I got you," he replied as he headed toward him.

He walked through the grass and grabbed the basket handles and went back towards the shack. He went through the door and sat the basket down on the edge of the quilt. He lifted the towel covering to find half a loaf of petrified cornbread and a lidded pot. He raised the lid off slowly and saw cold butter beans. He sighed and put his head in his hands and waited.

After a few minutes he heard the clanking of metal and raised his head up. Nehemiah walked through the door carrying a wood slatted bucket and two tin plates. He sat the bucket down and passed one of the plates over. Then he fished two spoons out of his back pocket and passed one over. Catawba sat the plate and the spoon in front of him while Nehemiah sat down.

"I'm not waiting on anything," Nehemiah said loudly.

He reached into the basket and broke off a big chunk of the cornbread and sat it on top of his kneecap. He took the pot out, pitched the lid back inside the basket, and poured a dollop of beans onto his plate. He handed the pot over to Catawba and he repeated the process. Then he put the pot back in the basket and broke off a piece of the cornbread too. He sat it on top of the beans and reached over and grabbed the jar. He passed the jar over to Nehemiah and he filled it to the brim.

They ate slowly and without speaking as the last dregs of sunlight disappeared behind the high mountains to the west.

When Nehemiah got through eating he grabbed the jar and chugged it. He filled it to the brim again and sat it back down.

"When you get done I'll take the plates and stuff back to the house. Just don't let me rush you."

"You're not rushing me. I'm done," Catawba said as he dropped his spoon onto the plate. "I can't eat much in this summer heat."

"I've got to eat. I need the strength . The reverend is always working me to death."

"Do you know what he had to do in town?"

"He lied," Nehemiah said as he stood up. "He told you town but he had to go up into the mountains for a spell."

180

"What? Why? Where did he go then?"

"He had to go see a man about some snakes. See, he believes in divination by serpents and preaching about prosperity. He says it's in the Bible. I don't hold to it myself but I listen to him. He gave me a place to live and a livelihood."

"Oh," Catawba replied.

Nehemiah bent over and gathered up the plates and tucked them back inside the basket. He picked it up and carried it out the door as Catawba sat motionless on the dirt floor.

He came back shortly thereafter carrying an old oil lamp. It had a smoke stained globe and its lighted wick danced with each step he took. He sat it down on the dirt floor and looked at Catawba.

"You haven't touched that water at all."

"I'm just not in the mood for warm water. I'd love to have anything cold though. Ice water or ice tea or an ice cold beer would hit the spot right about now. I'm always thirsty when it's hot out like this."

"Oh, I don't know about all that. The reverend wouldn't like it. Oh, and I forgot to tell you this when we were coming out here, but if you need to go to the bathroom just make for those trees right out back."

"I think I'll go do that."

He got up slowly and walked outside the cabin. The pasture land was bathed in darkness and the only light around came from a small bulb on the front porch of the farmhouse. He walked over to the edge of the woods and stopped. He stood there making water as a whip-poor-will called out from atop the ridge in front of him.

When he finished up he went back to the shack and sat down in the dirt. He looked at Nehemiah for a long time and then spoke.

"So you live here in this shack and eat cold food and drink warm water all the time."

"I usually get a hot meal come Sunday."

"What about bathing?"

"There's an old washtub and washboard in the barn. I make use of them when I get to smelling rank."

181

"Does this guy even pay you?"

"He gives me a little folding money on Saturdays when he gets back from the market, but he has to deduct for my living expenses. He'll most likely do the same to you too."

"We never talked about deductions but I don't care at this point. I'm starting to think this reverend is a wolf in sheep's clothing."

"Hey," Nehemiah said loudly, "don't talk about him like that. He is fighting the good fight against the evil of this old world. Where would any of us be without men like him?"

"I want you to think about what you just said. Think long and hard."

"What? What do you mean by that?"

"Think about it. Evil isn't working to corrupt the world; it doesn't need to. It's already corrupted the world and now all it has to do is corrupt the church and everything else will fall like grass before the scythe."

Nehemiah jumped to feet in a rage but calmed down in a flash when he heard the sound of the old truck coming up the gravel. Catawba turned toward the door and listened. The truck pulled up in front of the big barn and stopped. They heard the truck door slam, followed by the sound of footsteps, growing louder as they approached the shack. Catawba leaned back against the wall and waited. The reverend stepped into the shack and stood over the lamplight. He tossed the keys in the dirt at Nehemiah's feet and looked slowly back and forth at his two tired acolytes.

"I hope everything went satisfactory while I was away," he said in a low voice.

"Why yes it did, reverend. Catawba and me were just about to hit the hay for the night."

"Good Nehemiah. Did you feed our new helper?"

"I got the beans and bread out of the warmer box over the cookstove."

"That's good. Food does a body good. You alright Catawba? He didn't work you too hard did he?"

"No sir. I survived today and I'll be alive in the morning."

"Now that's what I like to hear. Now you boys say your prayers and hit the sack. We'll make an early day out of it tomorrow," he said as he turned around and walked out the door.

They heard the footfalls retreating up through the grass followed by the slamming of the screen door. Catawba raised his thumb tip and pointed it toward the farmhouse.

"You're never going to have a pot to piss in as long as you follow that man Nehemiah. I've lived around here my whole life and I know the type. They'll manipulate scripture and then use it as a cudgel to beat you into submission. And when you're beat down low enough they'll rifle through your pockets to get at your last nickel. He'll tell you that with backbreaking work and perpetual poverty you can earn your way into heaven but it doesn't work like that and it never did. He's no different than the people who are moving in here. We're going to end up beggars either way."

"I ought to go tell him what you're saying. He'll run your ass off from here. Besides, you're just mad you can't leave or do what you want while you're here."

"And neither can you Nehemiah."

"Yes I can," he said loudly.

"No you can't. You'll die right out there in that field hunched over a plow while the good reverend counts his loot from up there on that porch."

Nehemiah grunted and started hitting his head with the palm of his hand. Then he stopped and looked up at Catawba.

"I'll show you what I can and can't do. Just you watch," he said as he took off out of the shack.

Catawba grabbed the truck keys and stood up and peered out into the darkness. He couldn't see anything but he heard what sounded like brush breaking near the woodline. He listened to it until it stopped, then he sat back down and waited as the footsteps came back toward the shack. Nehemiah walked in carrying a green glassed demijohn in his hand. He sat down on the quilt, folded his legs up, and put the demijohn at his feet.

"What's in the jug?"

"Muscadine wine," he said as he shimmied out the cork. "I got it one day when I went with him to the farmers market. I put it behind the truck seat while he was talking to a customer and hid it in the woods when we got back."

When he finished talking he grabbed the quart jar and slung the remaining water out. He poured it full of the scarlet colored wine, took a quick glance at the door, and downed half the jar in one pronounced gulp.

"Here," he said as he held the jar out in front him.

Catawba grabbed the jar from his hand and took a big swig. He held it out in front of him and studied its bead against the light of the lamp.

" You be careful with that. It's potent and we're already dehydrated from today."

"Nonsense," he replied as he snatched the jar out of his hand.

He sat it back down and filled it again as Catawba leaned back against the wall and watched. He took another big swallow and passed the jar over. Catawba took it and drained half the jar without breathing. He sat the jar down on the quilt and wiped his mouth with the back of his hand.

"Let's leave in the morning. You can stay at my house and sleep on the couch. You can take a bath too. Then you can go out and find a job that doesn't make you sleep in the dirt and eat cold food."

"Really Catawba? Do you mean that ?"

"I don't see why not. You can get back on your feet and forget about this crazy place."

"I think I'll take you up on that," he said as he grabbed the jar and refilled it again. "I'll get up at first light and wrap my things up in the quilt and we can go. But first I'm going to go give that man a piece of my mind. I'm going to tell him he shouldn't be taking liberties with the unfortunate. It ain't Christian."

"Just let it go, Nehemiah. Letting go is the hardest thing to do there is. Trying to destroy evil by doing more evil is a very seductive temptation. I would know. It is one of my biggest weaknesses but at the end of the day you won't accomplish anything and you'll just end up miserable like me. Vengeance is just another stumbling block on the road to happiness."

184

"Hmm, that seems reasonable. But what do we do then?"

"Just let it go and one day we'll wake up to find that all the corrupt people in the world have destroyed themselves and we'll laugh like children."

"Let me think about that right there. Do you want some more?"

"I'm done and you should stop too. Let's just go to sleep and hit the road in the morning. We can take the truck to my house and drive it back here after we get my car."

Nehemiah looked over at Catawba for a moment and then stood up. He walked past him and disappeared into the darkness outside the shack. Catawba sat there in silence watching as the light of the lamp flickered up and down.

Nehemiah came back in a few minutes carrying a folded up blanket. He handed it over and sat back down.

" There's you a pillow to rest your head on," he said as he brought the jar up to his scarlett stained lips.

"Thanks," Catawba replied as he put the blanket on the ground behind him. "You didn't have to get it though. I could have made do."

"I had to go out anyway. I needed to check and see if there was gas in the barn."

"We could have got some in the morning. That way the truck would have been full when we brought it back. This place doesn't even have a phone so it's not like he can call the sheriff on us when we leave."

"Not the truck. I was checking the gas can. I wanted to make sure it still had gas in it."

"Well," Catawba replied as he put his head down on the blanket, "I think he'll be needing a lot more than gas once we leave."

"You hit the nail on the head there. Now get some shut eye . I'll wake you up before sunrise and we can head off."

"I think I'll do just that and you should too. Now finish off what you've poured and get some sleep."

Nehemiah reached over, took the globe off the lamp, and blew out the light. The inside of the shack became coal black and still.

"Goodnight Catawba."

"Goodnight Nehemiah."

30

Catawba woke up several hours later to the sound of screaming and the smell of woodsmoke. He jumped to his feet and stepped outside. The farmhouse was engulfed in flames and a man was crawling on all fours toward the barn. He took off running toward the man as fast as his feet could carry him.

When drew close he saw that it was the reverend. He was covered in soot and smoke rose up from his raiments. He collapsed and rolled over onto his back as Catawba ran up to his side.

"Tell me what to do to help you," he pleaded as he knelt down.

"That damn Nehemiah. He set my damn house on fire. I'll be waiting in hell for him, and you Catawba, you beautiful son of a..."

Catawba stood up and took off running back to the cabin. He went through the door and grabbed the handle of the wooden bucket and started back. The water sloshed over the sides with each uneven step he took. When he got within a few steps he lifted the bucket by the handle and bottom and flung all the water on the charred man. The clothes stopped smoldering but a faint vapor still rose up from his torso. He took two steps and knelt down at the reverend's head. He placed two fingers on the carotid artery and waited.

"Damn it," he whispered as he stood back up.

He took off in a slow walk toward the barn as he screamed out for Nehemiah. He stopped when he got near the truck and listened but heard nothing except for the sounds of cows bellowing and the crackling of fire. He consulted his pocket and brought out the key to the truck. He walked over, opened the door, and got in. He cranked it up and turned on the headlights and put it in reverse. Then he backed up until he was in the gravel of the driveway. He started turning the truck in slow circles, watching the headlights as they swept the darkened corners of the barn and fields and outbuildings.

He put the truck in park and rolled down the window. He listened for Nehemiah but heard nothing of interest. He tapped his fingers on the steering wheel a few times and then yanked the shifter into drive. He stomped down on the gas pedal and shot down the gravel and away from the raging inferno. He slid out onto the pavement and headed for home.

He had driven a few miles when he started to hear a muffled sound coming from the rear. He slammed on the brakes and listened. He heard it again and put the truck in park. He stepped out and looked into the moonlight bed of the truck. Nehemiah was lying on his back shrieking with laughter.

"You damn madman," Catawba said loudly. "Do you know they could get you for murder and arson? They'll put you and me in the penitentiary forever. I told you just to let it go."

"Yeah I know," he replied as he got up, "but I figured it another way."

"And what way is that?"

"I figured if I quit then the reverend would just go out and get someone else to work to death."

He jumped down and walked to the driver's side door and looked back at Catawba.

"I let the cows out after you went to sleep, if that's what you're worried about."

"I'm more worried about my freedom than the cows. Does anyone know that I was there?"

"Nope, nobody did. And only a handful of people knew I was there either."

"I'm not letting you stay at my house now so what do you intend to do?"

"I'm taking you home. Then I'm heading up into the mountains of Tennessee. I have some kinfolks up there."

Catawba nodded slightly and walked to the passenger's side and got in. Nehemiah climbed in too and they headed off. Catawba sat there in silence, looking out at the darkened trees as they appeared in the headlights and disappeared behind them.

An hour later Nehemiah turned off the blacktop. He parked at the bottom of the driveway and looked over at him. Catawba opened his door but didn't move.

"Do you need anything? I don't have much money but I could give you some clothes or some food."

"I'll be fine. I just need to get going. The darkness will be letting up soon and I want to make it to Sevierville way b efore noon."

"What are you going to do then?"

"Push this truck off in the woods where no one will find it. Then I'll walk to my brother's house. He raises sheep and goats. He'll put me to work I hope, though I haven't seen him in many years."

"Well," Catawba said as he opened the door, "I hope everything works out alright. I'll be taking this little adventure to my grave with me and so should you."

He stepped outside into the dark and slammed the door. He walked around the front of the truck looking in the windshield. Nehemiah gave him a small salute and then backed down the driveway and headed up the road.

Catawba stood there in silence watching as the lights of the truck disappeared. Then he walked up to the house and went inside. He headed down the hallway stripping off his clothes and shoes. He got in the shower and turned the water to scalding hot.

When he finished he got out and dried off slowly. He hung the towel up on the metal hook and looked at the clock on the wall, but it had stopped ticking, and it would never tick again, because for him time would be no more. He smiled as he walked out of the bathroom and turned on the coffee pot. He went to his dresser and got out clean clothes and put them on in silence. Then he walked back to the cupboard and got out a coffee cup. He sat it down next to the pot and stood there tapping his barefoot against the tile as it perked away.

When the coffee finished perking, he filled his cup full, and carried it out to the front porch. He leaned up against the porch column and listened for the owls, but they were silent and the land stood still. He stood there pondering the meaning of it all; oblivious to time and its ceaseless marching.

When the sun began to rise in the east he descended the porch steps and headed for the mailbox. He opened the lid and fished out a lone letter. He headed back up to the house tapping the letter against his thigh as he went. He climbed the steps, grabbed the cup, and headed inside. He put the cup by the sink and sat down at the kitchen table. He opened the letter to find two pieces of paper.

He unfolded the first piece of paper and read: I told you I would call the payroll office and have them take care of you. I even called the head honcho himself–Your friend Vance.

He smiled and sat the letter aside. He unfolded the second piece of paper to find a very sizable check personally signed by the director by the park service.

"Now we can get somewhere," he said loudly as he stood up and looked around.

He went to his bedroom, put on his best hikers, and threw some clothes in an old leather suitcase. He carried it out to the car and put it in the trunk. He went back inside the house and got his typewriter, paycheck, papers and other personal effects. He looked around for a brief second, then he cut the lights out and headed outside.

A few minutes later he pulled behind his grandfather's house. He got out and went inside the backdoor. The lights were out but he heard a faint crunching sound coming from the kitchen table. He flipped the lights on and saw his grandfather sitting at the table with a platter of cold bacon in front of him.

"Cut that light off," he whispered. "I don't want Dorothy to know that I am up."

"No," he replied. "Why are you eating that and why can't Dorothy know?"

"Because she makes me eat fruit and granola for breakfast. She said that's what they eat up north and up in the morning she forces me to get down on the floor and flop."

He stood there speechless as his grandfather shoveled the final strips of bacon into his mouth. He got up and carried the empty platter to the sink and sat it down. Then he turned around and wiped his mouth.

"Why are you looking at me like that?"

"She forces you to get down on the floor and flop?"

"Yes. She said it is good for my circulation and my brain. She does it with me too. I thought it was the silliest thing ever but my hip felt better after the first time I tried it. She said that if I feel up to it she'll sign us up for group classes in town. She drives good too. She even drove us around the lake the other day. Oh, and you really should mow your grass sometime because your yard looks horrible."

His chest grew tight as he watched his grandfather sit back down at the table. Then he rubbed his sinuses, sighed and opened his eyes.

"Pop, when you say she is going to sign you up for classes in town are you talking about that damn new fitness studio?"

"That's the place. How did you know that?"

"Because the other day I went on a hike to the top of the mountain with the woman who owns the place but I ended up having to hitchhike home."

"Why did you end up having to thumb home?"

"Because she stormed off and left me standing there."

"And why did she do that?"

"Because I put my stupid foot in my stupid mouth and she walked away."

"I've known you since birth and you've always been like that. You run your mouth to everyone you meet but one day you'll learn. You should go apologize to her. She is just doing what she thinks is best for the world. You can't fault a person for that."

"No, I guess not," he said slowly, "but I don't think that is ever going to happen; not today or next week or next year. I'm done with Fonta Flora. I received my final check from the park service and I'm going up into the mountains. I'm taking my typewriter and journal pages with me. You have Dorothy take care of you. Pop?"

"What?"

"Do you understand what I am telling you?

"What are you telling me?"

"I'm telling you that I may never come back here."

His grandfather stared at him for a few seconds and waved him over with his hand. Catawba walked over to where the old man was seated and stood. And the old man embraced the young man and the young man turned around and walked away and never looked back.

A few hours later he was sailing up the Blue Ridge Parkway with a slight smile on his face. The sunlight shone in from above and the cool wind blew through his hair.

He stopped at a little roadside cafe and had a late breakfast. When the waitress brought him the ticket she told him that he looked tired. "Yes," he replied, "and I'm going to find myself a cabin somewhere up the road and lay down and rest my tired soul." Then he got up and paid and went back to his car.

He drove on for many miles until he saw a faded sign for mountain cabins. He cut down the gravel road and headed for the office. He parked next to a thicket of rhododendrons in bloom and went inside the office to find a portly man seated like a statue behind the till.

"I'd like to rent a cabin for a while," he said as he walked up to the counter.

"Write your name down in the registry," replied the man leisurely.

Catawba took the chained fountain pen and jotted down the relevant information while the man got a key off the corkboard behind him.

"You can have the cabin on the far end of the property," he said as he laid the key down on the counter. "The cabin next to a creek. There's an old trail that runs up behind it. If you follow it up the hill you can look out over the valley below."

"Okay and how much do I owe you?"

"See if you want to stay here first. Our cabins are the bare essentials and most folks from the lowcountry don't like them. Those folks just can't live without modern conveniences. But if you do like it just pay us when you leave. You're the first customer we've had in quite a while. My name's Murphy."

"Thank you," he replied as he picked up the key.

"No problem young man. Now there's no refrigerators in the cabins. So when you get hungry you just walk right down here. You can eat with me and my wife if you're not too proud. We live in the back here."

"I think I'll take you up on that. I just don't want to leave for a while."

"If you don't mind me asking, are you running from something?"

"No. No sir. Sometimes you just need to get away to think straight."

The man nodded his head and Catawba turned around and walked outside. He drove down to the end cabin and got out. He walked over to the cabin door, unlocked it and disappeared inside. An old desk with a matching chair and a wrought iron cot were in the front room and nothing else. He walked to the bathroom and looked inside. He cut the light on and off and looked at himself in the mirror. Then we went back outside and carried his stuff in.

He put the suitcase at the foot of the bed and sat the typewriter and papers on top of the desk. He sat down and began shuffling through his journal papers. He arranged them in chronological order, slid them under the edge of the typewriter, and readied a blank piece of paper. "I'll start in the morning," he whispered as he stood up. He walked outside and headed for the small creek.

Little minnows, circumspect of humanity, darted away the closer he got to the creek. He stopped at the edge of the bank, closed his eyes, and listened to the ceaseless movement of the water. Then he bent down, cinched up the laces on his hiking shoes, and stepped across the creek and onto the footpath.

The narrow path was steep and overgrown with waist high sawbriars. He stopped halfway up the trail to catch his breath and dig the thorns out from under his skin. When he reached the top of the ridge he stopped and looked down at the ground. Little flakes of mica sparkled like diamonds against the moist mountain humus. He smiled and looked up and continued on. He weaved his way through a grove of oak trees until he found himself looking out over a small valley. He sat down and leaned his back up against a tree watching as flocculent clouds drifted slowly across the sky like wayward cherubs casting little shadows on the trees below.

192

He sat there for several hours enjoying the tranquility of the ridge until a big clap of thunder made him get up and head back. He got to the door of the cabin just as the bottom fell out of the sky. He went inside and sat down on the edge of the cot and peered out the small window of the cabin as the rain beat down on the tin roof overhead.

When the storm passed he got up and went outside and headed for the office. He walked through the door and stopped. The place was deserted. He heard voices coming from the room behind the counter so he walked over and knocked on the shut door. "Come in," Murphy called out. He opened the door and stepped into the cramped living quarters. Murphy and his wife were sitting at a small table looking at him.

"Alice, that's Mr. Fox," Murphy said as he looked at him, "the guest I told you about."

She got up from the table and walked over to him and shook his hand. She studied his face for a few seconds and smiled.

"Do you want something to eat? It's near past suppertime."

"That would be lovely."

"Well sit down and I'll be right back."

He walked over to the table and pulled out a chair. He sat down and looked over at Murphy.

"Is the cabin alright?"

"I have no complaints. The older I get the more I realize that having less means having more."

"Ha, you're touched in the head young man. Tell her," he said as stood up and pointed toward the cookroom, "tell her that I'm going to go check the locks on the cabin doors."

"I'll do that."

Murphy nodded his approval and hurried out of the room. After a few minutes she came back with a small plate and fork. She sat it on the table in front of him and stepped back.

"Cooked vegetables and mountain trout."

"Thank you so much," he said as he picked up the fork. "Your husband said he was going to go outside and check the property."

"That's his way of telling me that he is going to go outside to smoke. He thinks if he says it that way I won't worry about his health or get onto him about quitting. Some folks like to twist words to suit them."

"I know all about words. They've haunted me for years."

"I thought so," she replied.

She went back to the cookroom as he sat there eating in near silence. She came back when he was almost done and handed him a cup.

"Cold apple cider," she said as she sat down across from him.

"Thank you."

He took a long drink from the cup and sat it down on the tabletop while she sat there watching him.

"I went to your cabin while you were up on top of the ridge. I wanted to make sure you had a towel and a bar of soap in the bathroom."

"Thank you for that."

"I saw the typewriter and the paper on the desk. That is a most unusual thing for a man of your age to have."

"What do you mean by that?"

"I mean most of the people in your generation are usually more concerned with technology and money."

"I have never owned a smartphone and money has no bearing on me whatsoever. It's words that bother me. Do you know what I mean?"

"I'm not quite sure what you mean but you can tell me if you like."

"As most people get older they look back and resent the things they did or didn't do, but for me, I resent the things I said or didn't say. I lay awake at night and wonder what my life would have been like if I had said the right things to the right people at the right times but that's not the worst of it though. The worst of it is waking up one morning and finding out that your world has fallen apart and nothing you ever said or did mattered."

"I think we've all gone through that. It's part of the human experience. A person just has to move on and not wake the dead."

194

"That's the thing I can't do. My mind won't let it go. I'll start reading something or someone will say something and it all comes rushing back at me like a bull charging a matador. The vast majority of people think actions will change the world but that's not the case, only words can do that, and I can never find the right words."

"That's an interesting way of looking at life I guess."

"But that's now really the way I look at life though. I see life as a painting and words are the tiny brushstrokes that color in the fine details but I never have the right colors on my palette. That's the reason I'm here, at this place, I had to get away from it all to find the right colors for the picture."

"You can't paint the ocean while you're standing in a boat, is that it Mr. Fox?

"That's it in a nutshell I guess."

"Well," she said as she stood up, "you seem tired. Go get a good night's sleep and you can start in the morning. You'll have all the silence and solitude you need here."

"Thank you for this."

She smiled and gathered up the dishes and carried them back to the cookroom as he sat there in silence. He got up after a few minutes and walked outside. The mountain air was cool and a slight breeze came from the north as he walked back to his back cabin.

He stopped at the door, took a deep breath, and went inside. He kicked off his shoes, pulled off his socks, and climbed onto the creaking cot.

He laid there on his back looking up at the tongue and groove ceiling until the day died away and the sun retreated to the west.

As midnight approached he fell into a deep sleep and started to dream and in his dream he saw the faces of everyone he had ever known in front of him and the air became like a fiery furnace and the faces started to melt like candle wax and drip onto the bare floor. He took a deep breath and looked down at his feet to see a portrait of his entire life and in this portrait everything was perfect and the people were happy. He smiled as he knelt down to touch but then it was over. He woke up to discover that his youth had

195

fled from him like the dying of the spring and not all that glittered was gold.

He wiped the flowing tears from his eyes and stood up and walked across the room to the little desk and sat down and started typing. And as he typed…

He breathed a gentle word over the brook of life and realized that all things great and small run the river of time and empty out into the sea of our approaching eternity…

Made in the USA
Middletown, DE
27 October 2023

41369674R00120